Redeemer Chronicles 1: Awakening

By Julie C. Gilbert

Love Science Fiction or Mystery?

Choose your adventure!

Visit: http://www.juliecgilbert.com/

Dedication:

To Chewie, whose dare inspired this story.

Table of Contents:

Who's Who and What's What

Aeris – a planet created by Kailon

People Types:
Saroth – A people who live on the east side of Aeris's main continent. They are usually Gifted in the darker four of the seven magic schools and tend to become Destroyers, Shapeshifters, Conjurers, or Minders.
Arkonai – A people who live mainly in the northwest corner of Aeris's main continent. They are usually Gifted in the lighter three of the seven magic schools. Most Arkonai with access to magic become Seekers, Guardians, or Healers.
Bereft – Majority of people on Aeris who have no access to magic.

Other:
Victoria Saveron – Vic, the Lady's Chosen Redeemer
Kailon – Eternal King, Creator of Aeris
The Lady – immortal servant of Kailon

Key Saroth:
Marcus Polani – Katrina's father
Katrina Polani – Shapeshifter (beetle, dog, snake), Vic's friend
Jackson Castaloni – Conjurer, younger brother to Marina, older brother to Gabriel (deceased)
Gabriel Castaloni – Vic's dead uncle
Marina Castaloni – Vic's dead mother

Key Arkonai:
Daniel Saveron – Huntsman, Seeker, Vic's father
Tellen – Huntsman, Vic's friend
Jordan Lekros – Supreme Huntmaster, Shadow's father
Shadow – Huntsman, accepts a contract on Vic
Oren – Huntmaster, accepts a contract on Vic
Lerik – Oren's unofficial apprentice

Bereft:

Willem Baxter – Elder, native of Coldhaven, husband of Mary

Mary Baxter – villager, native of Coldhaven, wife of Elder Willem

Sara Andari – villager, native of Coldhaven

Ederon – villager, native of Coldhaven

Markesh McArn – Oren's follower, obsessed with Conjuring magic

Chapter 1:
Magic Bracers

Victoria Saveron
Temporary Camp, Foot of the Karnok Mountains
I suppose I shouldn't be surprised that my life has gone the way it has. Some people are just doomed. I—Victoria Amaryllis Saveron—am not a complainer, honest, but there comes a time when one has to examine the hand dealt by Fate and draw some conclusions.

My conclusion is this: life's not fair.

Let us examine the cards I've been dealt.

Cards one and two: a dark maternal heritage and a paternal legacy of eternal strife. Without going into the sob story, I'll simply say my parents' short love story and marriage wasn't exactly favored by the Saroth—Mom's folks—or the Arkonai—Dad's folks.

Marina Castaloni-Saveron—Mom—was a witch. I mean that in the most literal way possible. I'm not talking about a society of old ladies with bad complexions, creepy cats, and a depressing taste in clothes. I'm talking about an ancient and powerful, often dangerous, people with Gifts beyond this world. Mom was the black sheep, which means she secretly taught herself the healing arts and devoted herself to helping those in need.

Given that, naturally, Daniel Saveron—Dad—descends from the Arkonai, those proud guardians of the Bereft—those without magical powers. I asked him why they're called *Bereft* if they never had any powers to speak of. He grunted and said I'd understand one day. I really hate it when he says things like that. It makes me feel like a stupid child. Why can't he simply answer questions like a normal human

1

being? Never mind that he's not normal.

Cue sappy music.

Short version: Dad met Mom because he was tricked into hunting her by Uncle Jack, Mom's crazy younger brother. I'm told nearly everybody has a crazy Uncle Jack. Not sure I believe that, but I do know I have an uncle, his name is Jack, and he's definitely nuts and evil. Someday I'll have to ask him why he impersonated an Arkonai Huntmaster to put a hit on his sister. That's just wrong. It's no way to treat anybody, especially not somebody related to you. I don't have a sister, but I'm pretty sure I wouldn't hire somebody to kill her if I did.

After a patient hunt and rousing chase, Dad inevitably caught his prey, solved the mystery in time to avoid killing her, got past the whole awkward sorry-for-almost-killing-you phase, and successfully won her hand. That made nobody happy—except Mom. She was ecstatic to marry for love, though her former fiancé was rather put out, her family officially disowned her and put a bounty on her capture, and Dad's family snubbed her.

The Saroth are obsessed with bloodlines, lineage, and birth order, so they tried to arrange her marriage to Marcus Polani. Personally, I'm happy not being his daughter. Katrina Polani's a decent person, but she bit down hard on the whole I-am-better-than-everybody-else-because-I-have-magic Saroth nonsense.

With all the cheery goodwill going around, it's no surprise my parents fled to the woods to hide out, raise a family, et cetera. A horde of zombies attacked my parents when I was a cute, squishy baby. My parents prevailed in that fight, but Mom and I were both bitten. Why the blasted creatures bite is far beyond me. They carry supernatural swords, yet they insist on biting. It's so uncivilized. Stupid zombies. Then again, I'm not sure why they bother conjuring the swords since they always lose their arms.

Mom could heal herself or me, not both, so she saved me. I sometimes wonder what it would have been like if she'd saved herself instead. Of course, I wouldn't be around to see it, but she could have done so much more with her life. Dad found a powerful friend to make a pair of magical bracers that kept me from turning into one of those nasty little biters, hence the metal bracers—that often look like simple silver bracelets—and the thick leather gloves I wear. I don't really have to wear gloves on both hands, just the one that's gray and corpsified, but I find it less conspicuous to wear the pair.

Card three: I should be dead. The optimist in me says that

fact—namely that I'm not dead—is an accomplishment by itself, but the pessimist says that's only delaying the inevitable.

Card four: people want to kill me. It's not my fault I have two magical bloodlines within me. As far as I know, they've practically canceled each other out. Otherwise, I'd have cool powers like Katrina's ability to shapeshift or Tellen's ability to fry things with lightning.

What did I get? The most useless power ever. I glow when zombies or other dangerous or exceptionally powerful supernatural beings are near. The glow is not everywhere, thank goodness, but the whites of my eyes, my teeth, and my bracers light up like beacons if something possessing strong magical properties—especially dark ones—draws too close. These days, more often than not, that's when something is trying to kill me.

Card five: my two closest friends, Katrina and Tellen, hate each other. Hate might be too strong a word, but it's easier than saying they "have a strong aversion" to each other. I've already explained that Katrina's Saroth through and through, so as Fate would have it, Tellen's an Arkonai. He's an outcast among his people because of his destructive magical abilities, but that doesn't mean his upbringing didn't leave him with a well-developed prejudice against Saroth.

Dad says the idea that every Saroth delves into dark magic and every Arkonai sticks solely to light magic is complete rubbish. Though I hate to admit it, I think he's right. In any case, Katrina and Tellen are both cool with me because their masters—respectively, the great Saroth Shapeshifter, Talini, and the current Arkonai Supreme Huntmaster, Jordan Lekros—sort of ordered them to be my companions. I think they—the elders—know something they're not telling any of us.

Card six: I have no idea where the heck I'm going or how to get there. This whole crazy thing started when my father disappeared on another one of his hunts, leaving me with Katrina and Tellen. I sense a conspiracy. The first few days went fine. Then, yesterday we were having a nice game of darts when my bracers lit up, my eyes felt like they were on fire, and light poured from my mouth like airy drool.

Zombies came, zombies died, we swiftly packed parcels, and ran like cats with our tails on fire.

Card seven: I have a very uncomfortable feeling this is going to turn into one of those crazy quests to save the world. Since when did I sign up to be a hero? Somebody up there must have messed up the roll call.

Victoria Saveron -
Chosen Redeemer

Awakening

***

Katrina Polani
Temporary Camp, Foot of the Karnok Mountains

Vic looks worried. She tries to hide her feelings, but any Saroth with the smallest Minder capabilities could read her. I am uncertain about whether or not she knows where we are going. Some say quests must have an object or end goal in mind. For now, the goals are simply to stay alive and find Vic's father.

My young friend bears the mark of the Chosen Redeemer, but she does not yet realize it. I would like to tell her of the prophecy, but Father has forbidden it. I do not agree with him on this matter, but I shall honor the order for now. My ultimate task has always been to protect the interests of my people. Father has been meeting with the Dark Man again, and while he—Father—has a mind of his own, I fear the Dark Man's influence is growing. A time may come wherein I must tell Vic everything I know, but for now, I will keep silent.

Vic's marked for greatness, so she might as well have a large target painted on her head. Yesterday's attack confirms this, but I am just realizing what that means for me and my people. A world without zombies is a worthy cause to fight for, but destroying every link to the spirit world may destroy magic itself. I do not know what the Arkonai think about that, but my people will stop at nothing to prevent the Chosen Redeemer's coming if it heralds the end of magic.

As panic rises in me, I remind myself that nobody knows how the Chosen Redeemer will rid the world of the Darkland creatures. Destroying the link to the spirit world may not destroy magic. That is simply one possibility.

I wrench my thoughts away from my young friend's destiny back to the present. Poor Vic. She is not a subtle person. If she feels something or thinks something, her expression and demeanor will declare it. Her crystal blue eyes cannot hold a secret inside, and she does not have the luxury of turning herself into a bug to avoid confrontations. Perhaps that is why her father has not enlightened her. He was once very highly regarded among the Arkonai huntsmen. He might have even become Supreme Huntmaster if he had completed the contract on Vic's mother. Instead, he chose a different path. Despite this, he must know more than he has told my friend.

Since the initial clash with the zombies at Vic's home, we have avoided trouble. While this is good, I sense maleficent attention directed our way. I am not trained as a Minder, so for me to feel this sense of dread when thinking of Vic or our quest, something big must be happening. Vic did well in that fight, but she falls far short of the ideal warrior. For one thing, she does not like killing things, even the undead. Only crazy people enjoy killing things, but even the magic-less Bereft know there is a certain satisfaction one can draw from removing a zombie's head.

Interestingly, I do not believe Vic even knows she can fight well. Of course, I could not sit back and simply observe her in combat, but I believe she might have done most of her fighting with her eyes closed. She's an odd one, our Vic.

Normally, I know my role well. Kill this. Fetch that. Deliver a message. But this time I am uncertain whether I am to be guardian, guard, or childminder. I gaze around at the old trees rising up around us. The afternoon sun shines through clearly enough, but I know we will not be graced with its presence long. Though the weather remains hospitable enough to make foot travels easy, the night air will have a biting chill to it.

A Shapeshifter is never truly without a natural habitat, but the woods have always been regarded as an Arkonai realm to dominate. Tellen's off somewhere exploring, which suits me just fine. I do not trust the Arkonai boy. He claims to be here on orders from his master, but I do not trust his master either. I possess ulterior motives. I can only imagine what intricate plans have been conjured by the devious Supreme Huntmaster. Father has taught me to never underestimate any Arkonai. Personally, I find blood feuds pointlessly stupid. The world is dangerous enough without keeping the second most powerful people as close enemies.

Corruption has seeped in from somewhere. The Arkonai blame us, and I fear they are right. Though skilled fighters and in possession of mysterious powers, the Arkonai lack the keen interest in the arcane arts necessary to open Darkland portals. My people are usually not stupid enough to open those because they can be difficult to close, but sometimes ambition outpaces good sense.

Beyond the portals, fabled armies of undead await a mortal master's commands. The promise of power, though alluring, also comes with dire warnings of destruction. On the whole, my people could wage an effective war against the undead, but it would be a massive inconvenience. Vic would worry about the Bereft. No doubt the Arkonai would defend them to the last hunter, fools that they are.

The destruction of the Arkonai may be the intended plan. But who would be so bold? It has a certain level of creativity and elegant simplicity, but it still smacks of insanity. Only one bearing the Blessing of the Lady of Light could successfully control a large army summoned from the Darklands. Legends say the Lady of Light, goddess of good, loved a mortal man in ages past. Though she could not shed her immortality to be with him, she rained down blessing after blessing upon him. When war came upon the land—thanks to a previous zombie-happy crazy Conjurer—the Lady's mortal lover took up arms to fight.

In the final battle, the man fought brilliantly but was fatally wounded. Unable to stand his suffering and not wanting to watch him turn into a slathering creature someone would have to behead, the Lady of Light imbued the man's bracers with enough power to stave off the eternal night. In the process, she gave him enough power to control the army and send them back through the portal into the Darklands where they belong. The magic bracers were handed down generation to generation before being lost to time.

Few believe that fable, but it does sound eerily familiar. If the wrong people believe the story, it could mean a lot of trouble for us.

Chapter 2:
Katrina

Victoria Saveron
Temporary Camp, Foot of the Karnok Mountains

"Do not think so hard, you might hurt yourself." Katrina's comment catches me off guard.

I might have taken offense if she weren't more than half right. I pause and take a moment to reset the fire kindling on the stack of wood I've just arranged.

"I can't help it."

"What? No witty comment? You really must be worried." Katrina comes over and takes the flint and steel away. "Here now, let me handle the fire tonight. With you this distracted, you are as likely to set our bedding afire as boil the water."

Part of me wants to protest, but the rest of me is too tired to care. In seconds Katrina has a steady, safe fire burning strongly in the pit I've dug. She didn't need flint or steel because she's an all-powerful Saroth Shapeshifter, imbued with the ability to light fires with her mind.

I make a half-hearted effort to stave off the plunge into self-pity, but on par with the rest of my day, I fail. Dropping onto my blanket, I simply watch Katrina add some bits of this and that to the last of the rabbit she'd chased down yesterday. She's so gorgeous and powerful, and it makes me sick with jealousy.

Why couldn't the Fates have given me long, silky, dark hair that would allow me to blend in with the shadows? Instead, I got golden hair that tries to compete with any light source, the perfect target for even the weak sight and dim wits of zombies.

Even when she's not in her dog or snake form, Katrina's body radiates with lean, graceful power. I'll never understand Shapeshifters. As a dog, Katrina's fur is as black as bread after my attempts to toast it over an open flame. As a snake, her skin turns the same dusky shade as the dirt where she initiates the change. As an insect, she most often forms a red-brown flying beetle. As a human, she possesses skin several shades darker than mine. Her green eyes can pierce a soul at a glance.

"If you feel like unburdening yourself, I am here," Katrina assures. Even as she turns, she changes into a Labrador, pads over to me, and promptly invades my personal space, taking special care to draw near enough to pant in my face.

I laugh even as I hold both hands out to keep her at bay. I want to be cross with her, but it's virtually impossible.

"Yes, very authentic. You've been working on the dog breath, haven't you?"

Immediately, Katrina's back in her normal form though still crouched on her haunches and entirely too close.

"I have made several adjustments to it just today. Do you approve?" A teasing grin spreads across her face.

"Very authentic," I repeat cautiously.

Times like this confuse me. Katrina's usually dead serious, but there are rare occasions such as this where she's like a puppy eager to explore the world and earn approval. That image doesn't exactly suit the stoic Saroth Shapeshifter I've known since before I could stagger forward in a straight line.

"Excellent." With that, Katrina shuffles back to the cooking fire to attend the rest of the dinner preparations.

We have an odd relationship, Katrina and I. She's in my life because the Saroth don't trust me or my father. The same goes for Tellen because the same holds true for the Arkonai. My father encourages the friendships because it gives me something to focus on besides the fact that he's gone most of the time. He knows they report regularly to their masters, but even after the shoddy treatment due to his marriage to my mother, Father still fulfills his duties as an Arkonai huntsman. He used to have a much higher rank. Why he obeys fools he could best while blindfold, I do not know.

That brings me back to my worries.

"Why does he hunt? What does he hunt?" The questions

escape me before I can consider them.

The playfulness vanishes from Katrina's features. She hands me a bowl of stew and a spoon and studies me. After a long moment, she settles back into a more comfortable position and wraps her arms around her knees. Katrina stares forward into the dirt. When she finally speaks, her voice is softer and wearier than usual.

"Your father is a good man, but he is only one man."

"How are we going to find him if he's not in Coldhaven?" I ask, trying in vain to keep from whining. I don't really expect an answer. The emergency plan I never expected to use tells me to seek answers with the current elder of the nearest village. Father loves his cryptic games.

"When the time is right, he will come to us."

Katrina's still staring deep into nothing. Though I don't doubt my friend, I stifle the urge to kick her. Katrina is no Minder, but Saroth can be infuriatingly cryptic when they want to be, which happens to be most of the time. Sudden doubts grip me once again.

"Are we crazy? Should we have stayed at the cabin?"

"You are crazy-easy to sneak up on," scolds Tellen, "but we definitely needed to leave your zombie-infested home."

"Hi, Tellen," I greet him.

"We knew exactly where you were," Katrina insists calmly. "Your odor preceded you as usual." She glances up to see if the insult will get a rise from Tellen.

He grunts and tosses a mock scowl at Katrina.

"And here I was going to share this grand treasure I found, but if you'd rather I keep the blueberries to myself—"

"Blueberries!" I might have squeaked a little. They're my favorite, and they never grow in the bushes around my home.

"Are you sure they are not baydonberries again?" Katrina inquires. "It is not exactly the right season for blueberries."

The thought quenches some of my enthusiasm.

"I'm never going to live that one down, am I?" Tellen groans.

"Nope," I answer, forcing a weak smile. My stomach clenches at the thought of the disastrous surprise he'd given us about a year ago. Baydonberries look almost exactly like blueberries, except that they have tiny white flecks in the fleshy part. They taste almost the same too. Unfortunately, they have amazingly thorough *cleansing* abilities. I think I puked up everything but my intestines and then had other unpleasant side effects for two days.

"People tend to remember when you almost kill them," Katrina points out.

Katrina Polani - Saroth Shapeshifter

"These are the real thing," Tellen insists. "Look." He reaches into his pocket and draws forth a fat, luscious berry. "I'll prove it."
With a flick of his wrist, Tellen flings the berry up into the air and moves to catch it in his mouth.

Faster than I can track, Katrina turns into a snake, coils, and springs, intercepting the berry mid-flight. She spits it at the fire where it explodes with a force strong enough to knock Tellen back a step.

"Whoa!" Even in the flickering firelight, Tellen's skin looks paler now.

Back in human form, Katrina frowns, looking both surprised and annoyed with herself for intervening.

"You really should leave the berry hunting to Vic."

I agree, but I'm too stunned to speak. My mouth just opens and closes for a while. Normal baydonberries will briefly turn a flame a deep purple color, but I've never heard of one exploding.

"Perhaps you should remove the rest from your pockets," Katrina suggests.

Tellen fumbles in his right pocket, only too eager to comply. In his haste, he drops another one into the fire. It bursts into flames, causing a shower of sparks to fly out at us. I duck instinctively, dunking my chin into my stew bowl. Setting the bowl aside, I brush my chin with the back of my hand, hoping nobody saw that.

While I recover my dignity, Katrina assumes her snake form and curls into a defensive coil. She stays like that for three heartbeats beyond the last spark's death before returning to normal.

"Where did you find them?" I ask.

"Just over there," Tellen says, pointing back up the way we'd come this afternoon. "Behind that outcropping. There must be hundreds of them up there."

"Show me," orders Katrina. The next instant she's a dog on high alert. Her ears perk up and her muscles tense. She barks and nips at Tellen's heels to let him know she means business.

Tellen looks like he wants to protest, but the cold glint in Katrina's eyes convinces him resistance would be futile—and possibly painful.

"Stay here," he orders me, before taking off at a sprint.

Stay here by myself with a dying fire. Uh, no, not a chance.

Weariness flees me as I leap to my feet, put out the fire, and race after my friends.

12

Chapter 3:
Tellen

Katrina Polani
Path to the Baydonberry Patch

Is he dumb or devious or something else entirely? Tellen could hardly have meant us harm if he tried to eat the first berry himself. Did he know I would intercede? Part of me wishes I had not bothered intercepting that evil fruit. The baydonberries Vic and I ate last year certainly made us violently ill, but this would have been far worse. One may not have killed Tellen, but getting sick would serve him right.

I do not mean that. I wish I did, but I cannot bring myself to hate him. I put up a good front so Vic will not know of my true feelings. As I have mentioned, if Vic knows something, the world knows it soon thereafter. Truthfully, I do not know if I understand my feelings toward Tellen.

He is loyal to Vic, but he keeps to himself. Like all Arkonai huntsmen, he comes and goes as he pleases, though if trouble comes he will likely be present to lend aid. His people and mine share the loner status. Despite their flaws, the Arkonai always honor their contracts. The same cannot be said for my people, but then again, Saroth rarely hire out their services. We do as we like when we like. While a freeing philosophy, I can see where this attitude has gotten us into trouble in times past and how it may bring more trouble soon.

A thick branch appears before me and I barely duck in time to avoid a serious headache. Master Talini always said to focus on the

13

chase while in dog form. She rarely uses dog form, preferring to be a hawk for traveling purposes. I wish I could turn into a flying creature such as a hawk, but Master Talini refuses to teach me the skill. She thinks me unready for the unique challenges of true flight.

In truth, I sense Father's influence at work in the reluctance. He probably fears I'll get myself shot by some ignorant Bereft hunter out to prove his prowess with a bow and arrow. While a legitimate fear, I do not subscribe to his logic. After all, Master Talini taught me how to become a beetle. I would wager my human form weight in gold that the danger of being maliciously squashed under a boot far exceeds the threat of a thrill hunter's arrow.

Tellen halts abruptly in front of me. I take my snake form because it has a quicker reaction time. Unable to halt my forward momentum, I throw my body upward and right, looping thrice around the tree next to Tellen.

"We should—"

An arrow zips toward Tellen, causing him to abandon the rest of his statement. He drops into a crouch and draws the twin daggers from the sheaths at his waist. Three more arrows slam into the tree I occupy. I turn myself into a beetle and tremble with suppressed rage. I could have been pinned to that tree for the rest of my short life had those arrows found their mark.

Using the energy from the anger, I fly further up into the tree, turning back into a human only once I am perched high above the would-be battleground.

Vic arrives belatedly and stares incredulously at the three arrows in the tree next to Tellen. Then, her eyes start glowing. She clamps her mouth shut to keep the light from her teeth inside, but the effort is wasted because her bracers do their magic thing. Normally, Vic's bracers take on a thin form that looks like a pair of gaudy, silver bracelets, but if powerful magic approaches they consume her forearm from wrist to elbow and blaze with blinding light.

"Get down!" Tellen hisses.

Before Vic can move, two zombies appear with greedy arms outstretched as if to embrace my slight friend. I wince as Vic's scream echoes down the mountainside. If there are other enemies in the area, they now know exactly where to find us.

Tellen's daggers flash several times in the light streaming off of Vic, quickly dispatching the zombie attackers. Decayed arms and legs thud to the ground.

Four right fists pierce the ground simultaneously, surrounding Vic. Then, time slows as one after another of the new zombies drag their bodies from the disturbed soil and reach for Vic from every side. She ducks under swinging arms—and glowing swords—and weaves in and out of danger almost quicker than my eyes can track.

The swords carried by the undead are not natural weapons. They can cut through flesh, bone, and spirit. Generally, zombies can be easily defeated, but their swords make them dangerous, for a small nick can sap one's will to fight as surely as a sweeping, mortal wound.

One particularly bold zombie launches himself at Vic, mouth open to tear into her. Instinctively, she whips her right forearm up to intercept the eager teeth. The zombie chomps down on Vic's bracer then howls with pain. The desperate cry momentarily baffles the other attackers.

The distraction is exactly what Tellen and I need to dispatch the remaining zombies. Tellen buries both daggers in the nearest zombie's chest while I turn to my snake form.

Dropping onto one attacker's head, I wrap myself tightly around its neck before leaping toward the next one. As I reach the next zombie, I release the first's head. The neck snaps with a satisfying crunch. In a similar manner, I wrap around the second zombie's head then leap to the tree where I had first dropped down. As I prepare to dispatch the last zombie, I see further intervention is unnecessary. The zombie that bit Vic's bracer stands like a statue, face twisted in agony and arms held wide as if he would hug her.

Vic stares up at the creature invading her personal space. She looked even younger than one who has recently reached her teens.

Tellen reaches out a cautious finger and touches the zombie in front of Vic. It crumbles into ash and blows away on unholy wind.

For a long moment, nobody moves.

"What just happened?" Tellen asks, voicing the thought that had jammed itself inside my head and refused to come out.

In animal form, I can sometimes tap into extra senses. I felt more trouble the instant before another three arrows flew at Vic. A warning cry dies in my throat as Tellen's eyes widened and he raises a hand toward Vic. Worry nearly crushes my lungs.

Time slows again and Vic's mysterious powers take over once more. This time, she stands firm, glowing from the bracers, mouth, and eyes. Calmly, she forms fists, holds them side by side in front of her face, and leans forward as if to rest her head on them. Then, she throws back her head, shuts her eyes, and makes three grabbing motions. Each grasp results in her plucking an arrow out of flight and flinging it back at its source.

I know not what expression I wore, nor even what form I had at the time, but Tellen nearly dropped his precious daggers. Luckily for us, Vic's aim was true, and the three zombie archers fell in a neat row with arrows in their foreheads. Their pale, gray skin stretches tight over gaunt, emaciated features which are locked in grimaces. Even in real death, they look angry with Fate. The three archers had the few scraps of tangled black hair tied back with leather cords, forming ponytails high on their otherwise smooth skulls.

The light vanishes from Vic and she collapses in a heap, making me think another arrow had somehow breached her scary defenses. Dropping to the ground beside my friend, I reach out to touch her cheek.

She wakes up in time to catch my hand then yawns mightily.

"Did I miss something?"

"Small brawl with zombies; nothing important," Tellen assures her.

Struggling to sit up, Vic glances around.

"Are you sure it wasn't a dream?"

I exchange a glance with Tellen then nod at Vic.

"How come I always faint during combat?" Vic wonders.

"This is only the second fight we've been in," Tellen reminds her. He pauses to help Vic to her feet. "Give it time. I'm sure there will be plenty of fights ahead."

I pierce the idiot with a glare.

"That isssssssss sooooooo reassssssssuring."

Vic turns to me, amused.

"I didn't know you could talk as a snake."

Returning to my human form, I say, "It takes more concentration than usual to speak while in an animal form. Most Shapeshifters do not bother, but this is hardly the time for idle chatter. We should leave. This place is evil."

By this time, the zombies had disintegrated.

"I thought you wanted to check on the baydonberries." Tellen waves around us. "Here's your chance."

The area around us brims with baydonberry bushes.

"No, that's okay," Vic says swiftly. "My curiosity's satisfied."

Though we survived without a scratch, my interest is piqued. Why did Tellen lead us here? Certainly he killed some of the creatures, but he could also be complicit in summoning them in the first place. One would need a powerful artifact or a willing Saroth Conjurer to create that many zombies. What was the point?

"Suit yourself, but I'm curious. I'm going to take some to study later." Taking a small pouch from his belt, Tellen carefully gathers berries from several different bushes.

"Hurry," I say, "we should return to camp and rest. We will need to push hard if we want to reach Coldhaven by tomorrow evening."

With his task finished, Tellen starts down the path toward our camp.

I sense someone—or something—watching us, but Vic already looks ill with unease so I keep the fact to myself.

Chapter 4:
Grander Games

The Lady
Ruins of the Earth Temple, Neutral Ground
Tremendous power often carries an unexpected price.

I cloak my presence from the hooded figure patiently awaiting the Supreme Huntmaster's arrival. I do not need to see Jackson Castaloni's face to know he resembles the dead more than the living. His pale skin bears more wrinkles than it ought to for a man his age, and his dark eyes appear perpetually tired.

If he knew I could see into his dark heart, read his surface thoughts, and witness his secret meeting, he would take measures to neutralize my efforts. Though he can hardly hurt me directly, Jackson knows enough to hurt that which I deem most precious. I fear my efforts to curb his ambitions have proven quite futile.

Though Jackson's mind cannot be influenced, I am not without resources. The current resource—Alec Castaloni—hardly leaves his master's side. As an inquisitive child and Jackson's apprentice, Alec makes a lovely conduit for my questions.

"Uncle Jack, why are we here? Why is the head huntsman coming?" The boy's voice rings with crystal clear innocence.

I feel the flash of anger burn deep within Jackson, but it dissipates quickly. As the son of Jackson's dead younger brother, Alec may be the one person the Saroth Conjurer cannot stay angry with.

To my disappointment, Jackson merely grunts, and says, "Quiet, boy, watch and learn, and when the Arkonai arrives, keep silent."

"*I know only that the Denkari are not the worst Jackson Castaloni can - and will - summon if given half a chance.*"
~The Lady

Despite my eagerness to press the point, I dare not risk arousing Jackson's anger this early in the day. He loves the child to distraction, but he often takes discipline too far. I may not be above using a child to voice questions, but I will not become a cause for that child to be beaten.

"If you'll not answer the question for the boy, answer it for me," says a voice from the shadows. Supreme Huntmaster Jordan Lekros calmly rises from a crouch and steps into the light of the lantern Jackson has set up in the center of the massive stone table. The table and the nine crumbling pillars arranged in a circle around it are the only remains of an ancient temple honoring Kailon for the fertile earth and abundant harvests.

Surprise blossoms within Jackson but the hood hides his expression. He deepens his voice as he intones, "You are late."

"And you are wasting my valuable time," returns Jordan Lekros. "State your business."

"I have a mutually beneficial proposition," Jackson promises.

"You have nothing I want." The Supreme Huntmaster's face is inscrutable, but I sense his impatience.

"I know much about you that even you do not." Jackson has no intention of revealing his knowledge right now, but the thought surfaces in his mind, allowing me access to it.

My surprise at the revelation causes Alec to flinch, but the men are too intent on their verbal dance to notice.

"I am a simple man," Jordan Lekros declares. "I have few secrets and fewer still to care if they're revealed, so if it's blackmail you—"

"Far from it," Jackson practically purrs. "For example, I know that you and I share a goal." He pauses to give the Supreme Huntmaster a chance to inquire, but only silence answers him.

"Tell him, Uncle Jack," Alec urges at my prompting.

The interruption earns Alec an icy glare, but Jackson complies.

"You and I both want to punish the Saverons for the past."

The Supreme Huntmaster's expression remains impassive, but for the first time his voice carries a hint of interest in the conversation.

"Daniel Saveron is a good man. I do not wish him dead, and Victoria is an innocent."

He lies. He does wish Daniel Saveron's death, though his surface thoughts do not reveal why.

A mixture of revulsion and loathing sweeps through Jackson,

but no trace of these emotions reaches his voice as he tries to set the Supreme Huntmaster's mind at ease.

"I bear the girl no ill will. She is my niece, after all. My sister, misguided though she was, carried the blood of my family within her."

"You had your sister murdered," Jordan Lekros states flatly.

"There's no—"

"There's no need for proof when everybody knows the truth." The Supreme Huntmaster levels a steely gaze at Jackson. "I have better things to do than hear you prattle about the past. Reports of undead attacks are increasing. If I find you're responsible, I will kill you."

"I am but a humble Conjurer. It would take far more power than mine to raise so many undead. Indulge me a moment longer, and you will know how I can help both of our peoples."

The Supreme Huntmaster nods curtly and scoffs at Jackson's false modesty. Lekros stands stiffly, his posture reflecting his reluctance to hear Jackson's proposal.

Undaunted, Jackson says, "You have a problem, my friend. You cannot kill Daniel Saveron without more than half of your people turning against you."

"I told you I do not wish his death!" The force and raw anger in the exclamation support his words, but the cold cast to his glare contradicts them.

"We both know that is a lie. Daniel brought shame upon your people by mixing the magic lines, a dangerous thing to be sure. Victoria is hardly the threat spoken about by prophecy, but if nothing is done, more people will be emboldened to break the healthy taboo we've cultivated for centuries."

"My people won't hunt him," Jordan Lekros admits. The finality in his voice tells me he's given the matter much thought.

"Ah, but your people can make a clean capture. Bring my niece to me." Jackson raises a hand to forestall the obvious protest. "I swear not to harm her. I simply wish to hold her until her father surrenders."

"I'm not condoning the use of a thirteen-year-old girl to bait a trap." Despite the words, I detect a strange excitement and triumph streaming off the Supreme Huntmaster.

"Think of the benefits. Your problem will be dealt with and your hands will be clean."

"What do you get out of this deal?" Lekros asks, not bothering to mask his suspicion.

"In addition to restoring my family's honor, I will be doing my part to prevent the end of the world. Does a man need more reason to act?"

"Most men may not need more reason, but you are not most men. You always have a reason."

Jackson laughs.

"Indeed I do, but you need not concern yourself with that."

"If it involves one of your schemes, it will likely concern me later, so I'd rather hear it now," Lekros insists. "Take off your hood. If you want my help, look me in the eyes and tell me the truth."

A battle rages within Jackson, but he finally agrees. Slowly, he reaches up and removes the hood. His face has withered since my last glimpse of him. His eyes have sunk deeper into his face, making his cheekbones more prominent.

Supreme Huntmaster Lekros draws in a quick breath. Horror and revulsion has him reaching for a dagger before he masters the surprise.

Jackson glares defiantly.

"So you know my secret. I have slowed the poison with my powers, but only one thing can save me."

This statement confuses me, for I know not why Jackson Castaloni wishes his condition blamed upon a zombie bite when it stems from a different source entirely.

"You promised not to harm Victoria."

The Saroth Conjurer's smile is cold and cruel.

"And I won't, but once her bracers are removed, she will cease to be herself, leaving me no choice but to kill her. When that happens, even your people will beg to be in on the hunt."

A storm of conflicting emotions within Jordan Lekros distracts me. Only one thing is clear to me, he wants the bracers for himself, but I cannot fathom why. His magical abilities are not suited to using the bracers, yet his mind buzzes with a strong sense of possession.

Released from my hold, Alec rushes forward.

"No!" Anguish fills the boy's voice as tears course down his rosy cheeks. The sun has now risen and shines fully on his angelic features.

"Silence," orders Jackson.

"Let him speak," says Lekros.

Alec struggles against sobs. Short of breath, he swallows hard and shouts, "Not Vic!" Reaching his uncle's side, Alec clings to

Jackson's robes. "Please, don't kill Vic." Each word emerges like a full speech.

I feel Jackson's rage mounting like a deep ocean storm. Risking much, I marshal my powers and soothe the child into silence.

"This is madness," Jordan Lekros comments. "I cannot believe I'm even considering this. I don't even know if it can be done. Victoria doesn't deserve such an end." Despite his words, the Supreme Huntmaster's mind hums with pleasure. Even though he will delegate the hunt to someone else, he relishes the thought of it.

Sensing victory, Jackson presses his case.

"You bear the burden of leadership, as do I. How do you think I feel? She is family! Still, I stand a better chance of using those bracers to their full-effect and stemming the tide of rising undead than an untrained girl!" He pauses to let his words set in and removes the traces of passionate panic from his tone before adding, "Many will die if we do not take this distasteful path. Will you help me?" After another significant pause he adds, "You can have the bracers once I'm done with them. I know you seek them."

"We cannot both have them," Lekros points out. "You'll turn."

Shaking his head, Jackson says, "I only need them for a time to reach the power behind the Veil. Then, you can keep them."

Lekros wants to believe Jackson, but like me, his suspicions remain high.

Chapter 5:
Shadow

The Lady
Supreme Huntmaster's Office, Castle Cardeth

As he waits for his son's arrival, the Supreme Huntmaster considers his meeting with the Saroth Conjurer. He doesn't like the plan they formed together, but the alternatives appeal even less. The number of undead sightings grows daily. If the alarming trend continues, his people will be hard-pressed to protect the Bereft.

Standing in front of the window, Jordan gazes out at the flickering firelight from the courtyard lanterns. Since the lanterns in his office are kept very low, darkness surrounds him. Oddly enough, he finds it comforting.

As much as it galls him, he admits that Jackson Castaloni understands the situation perfectly. The Arkonai people will never allow a contract to be written for Daniel Saveron, especially not after he has started fulfilling contracts again. Nothing had been done in the twelve plus years since the attack that killed Marina Castaloni-Saveron and wounded young Vic.

Unease runs through Lekros at the thought of sending Shadow after Vic to get to Daniel. He knows it's a cowardly move, one for the greater good to be sure but still cowardly. Had Jordan been stronger back then, he would have challenged Daniel to a death match to restore his people's honor. Now that he is stronger, the moment has long since expired.

The thought of leaving magical bracers in Jackson Castaloni's hands deepens Jordan's unease. The Conjurer may claim noble intentions, but there has to be more to his motivation than the desire to prevent himself from becoming one of the undead. Longstanding tradition alone dictates he have a deeper, darker desire lurking in his mind.

Shadow's experience pales in comparison to his more seasoned colleagues. Castaloni argued specifically for Shadow, citing the need for a low-profile hunt. One would think that a society of hunters must be good at keeping secrets, but rumors fly just as swiftly, perhaps even quicker among the Arkonai than among village people.

The cynical part of Lekros applauds the genius of the move from the Saroth's point of view. He had not given serious thought to a double cross, but now with his son's reputation—and perhaps even his life—on the line, he has even more reason to see the mission succeed.

"You summoned me, Supreme Huntmaster," says Shadow formally.

Years of training keep traces of surprise and alarm locked inside. Jordan Lekros doesn't like that Shadow's approach went undetected, yet fierce pride fills him at the boy's mastery of stealth. The Supreme Huntmaster turns slowly to face Shadow and clears his throat so his voice will be steady and strong. "I have a contract for you. It is there on the table for your consideration."

Shadow gestures toward the parchment and it obediently flies to his outstretched hand. A brief touch and some whispered words cause the pendant hanging from his neck to glow, giving him enough light to peruse the paper.

I try to get a sense of Shadow's mind, but I meet impressive mental walls. Perhaps my powers have truly atrophied, or perhaps I am simply not meant to know much about this black-clad, slight young man. For some reason, I know he has a role to play in the future, but the impression is meaningless without context.

Lekros suppresses the desire to scold Shadow over his casual use of magic. Casual use can lead to disrespect for the art, a cheapening of the gift Fate had bestowed upon the Arkonai. The Supreme Huntmaster says none of this, for he does not wish to further alienate the boy by treating him like a first-year apprentice. For a brief moment, he fights the impulse to step forward, rip the black cloth away from his son's face, and gaze upon him. He wonders how long it's been since he last looked upon his child's face.

As waves of longing threaten to become a dangerous distraction, Lekros pushes aside his reservations about Arkonai tradition. He understands and believes in the wisdom of keeping family connections distant. When he chose the path to become Supreme Huntmaster, Jordan relinquished family ties to his pregnant wife to protect her from ambitious rivals. The memory of Christa's hurt expression stabs Jordan even as he consciously tries not to think about her. Since that time, he's seen her only once when she came to present the child to the elders for blessings. Clearing his mind, Jordan focuses on arguments Shadow may bring up and how to answer them.

"This is not right," murmurs Shadow.

Pulled from his reverie, Lekros wishes somebody had taught the boy to speak boldly instead of this sibilant speech that requires one to strain to hear. "It is necessary."

"I know this girl and her companions. They are no threat. Why do you wish this done?"

Sighing, Lekros considers how much to reveal.

"The bracers the girl wears could be the key to closing the Darkland Portals through which these infernal beasts are seeping."

"Then ask for her aid."

The ridiculous notion strikes Lekros as funny, but he suppresses the mirth.

"She is young and lacks the necessary power."

Stony silence meets this declaration.

Knowing he's offended Shadow, Lekros holds out a hand in a placating gesture. Then, a disturbing thought strikes him.

"You're not in love with the girl, are you?"

Shadow barks a harsh laugh.

"Would it matter if I was?" He waves off an answer and continues, "No, Father, but you are underestimating her."

"Do you doubt your abilities?" Lekros wonders, confused by Shadow's continued reluctance.

"I *can* do it. I'm not convinced I *should* do it."

Deciding on a different tact, Lekros appeals to the boy's ego.

"You're the only one I trust with this, Devin."

Shadow stiffens at the use of his given name.

Slowly, Jordan Lekros reaches out and places a bracing hand on his son's shoulder. "As the contract says, it is for 'capture' only. Bring me the girl so I can give the bracers to her uncle until he closes the portals. Then, we will restore them to her. You have my word on that."

The dim light from Shadow's pendant casts only enough light to reveal the lower part of his masked face, but Jordan feels the intensity of his gaze.

"And her companions?"

"What of them?" Lekros asks.

"The contract speaks of the girl's fate, but they will not abandon her."

"If possible, give them to the girl's uncle so he can think he controls her, but if they become too much trouble, deal with them as you see fit." The Supreme Huntmaster avoids ordering the death of the girl's companions, for he knows Shadow will not approve.

Shadow's disapproval gets aired anyway.

"Tellen is Arkonai."

"True, and the Polani girl is Marcus's daughter. Jackson Castaloni will not harm them without cause."

"He will betray you," Shadow whispers.

"I know," Lekros replies as a surge of pride sweeps through him. "I'm looking forward to it, but that should not lead to death for the other youths if that's what you're worried about." He removes his hand from Shadow's shoulder before the urge to crush the boy in a hug can overcome his dignity.

Silence falls between them as Shadow considers various arguments, and Lekros silently prays the young man will trust him to handle these dangerous political games.

"You want a war," Shadow says at last.

The statement takes the Supreme Huntmaster aback but he recovers quickly. Making a decision to trust his son, he says, "The Saroth are dangerous. The world will be better without them."

"But where does it end?"

"What do you mean?"

Shadow lays the parchment on the side table where it came from and paces, gathering his thoughts. Lekros lets him, knowing that the boy must be willing or the contract will not be fulfilled. Finally, Shadow leans back against the far wall and crosses his arms over his chest.

"What do you intend, sir?"

"The reasonable Saroth who surrender will be spared, and the wayward Arkonai can be reformed," Lekros replies, disappointed in the weakness of his son's argument.

Pushing himself off the wall and unfolding his arms, Shadow once again reaches out and snatches the contract out of the air.

"I will take the contract."

The sudden reversal leaves Jordan Lekros elated but suspicious. He does not believe the boy will betray him, but perhaps a secondary contract is in order.

Shadow

Chapter 6:
Ghostly Visitor

Victoria Saveron

Temporary Camp, Foot of the Karnok Mountains

Nobody enjoys feeling helpless, but that's exactly the emotion I've been drowning in for days, even before the first attack. I hate that it makes me sound needy, but honestly, the feeling of dread has followed me since my father left five and a half days ago.

Neither Katrina nor Tellen will tell me about the recent fight. I can draw my own conclusions from the disgusted way Katrina keeps shaking her fur in her dog form.

I wouldn't even have remembered there was a fight if my tingling teeth didn't remind me. I'm told some people have the unique ability to block out traumatic events, but I find it plenty traumatic to awaken amidst the cold ashes of recently vanquished undead. I am trying hard to not freak out, but so far my success is only marginal.

My appetite died with the zombies, but now that Katrina's finished with her self-cleaning rituals, she calmly rebuilds the fire and reheats my portion of the stew. Since I lack the energy for a rousing fight, I meekly accept the bowl, thank her, and eat without tasting anything.

Tellen's off gathering more firewood so we don't have to do that in the middle of the night. He's under strict orders to not bring back any edible surprises. Each sizzling crackle of firewood has me flinching as I think about the exploding baydonberries. A deep desire to make myself useful goes only so far as the inconvenient thought of having to leave my blanket.

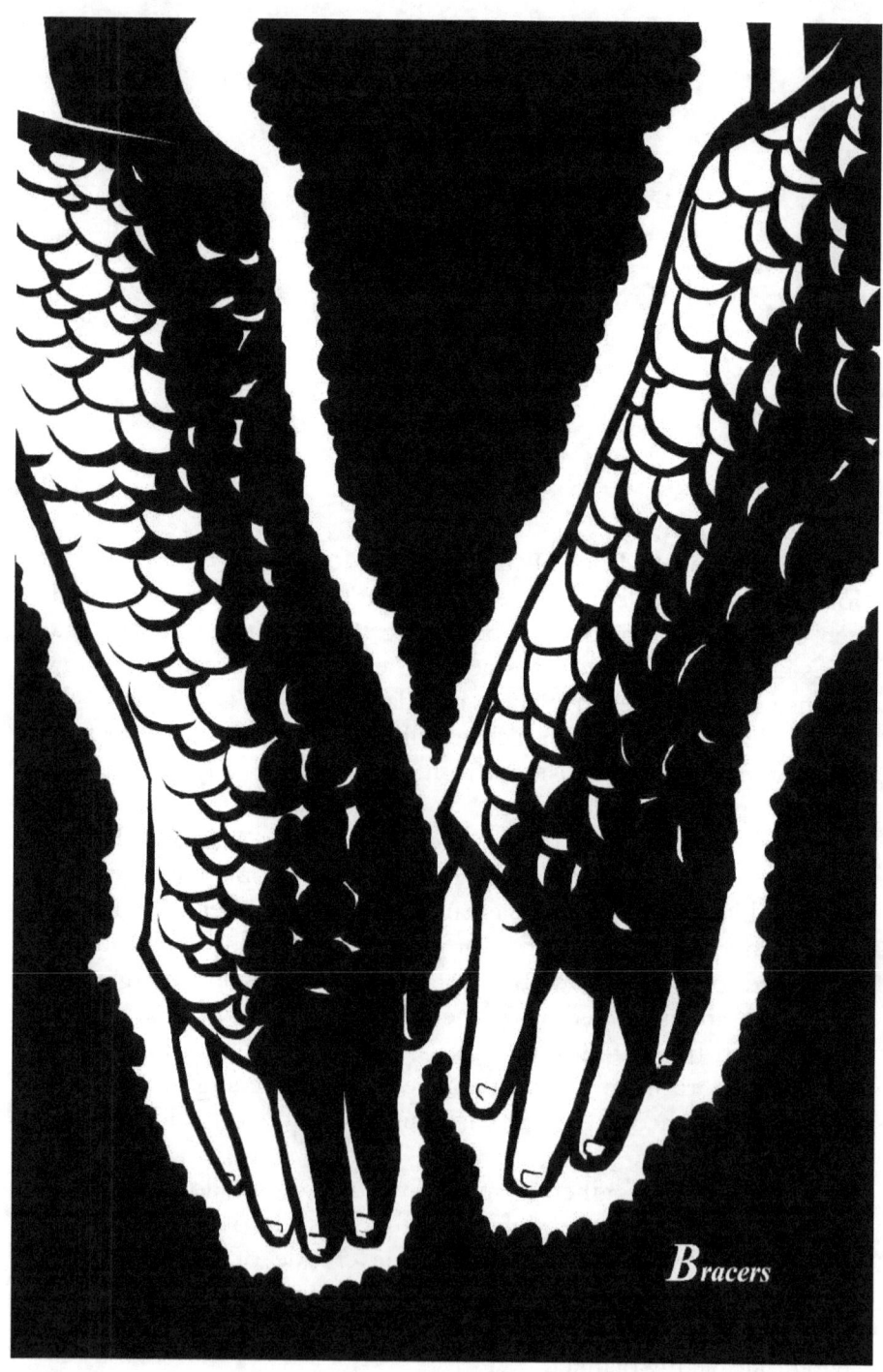

Bracers

To distract myself, I study my bracers. They're the thinnest I've ever seen them. The tiny etchings that sometimes look like fish scales are now tighter, giving the illusion of finely woven threads. They confuse me. Most of the time, I can remove them if I want, though there have been a few troubling times in my life when that was not the case. Usually, the bracers look like ordinary bracelets, but whenever I reach a certain level of unease, they morph into sleek bracers as hard as steel swords. I'm tempted to remove the bracers for the sense of freedom.

"Do not even think about removing those," Katrina scolds. For someone who claims no Minder capabilities, she reads me quite well.

Heeding her words, I quit fiddling with my bracers and slip into my thoughts.

"What are you thinking about?" Katrina asks, noticing my attention has wandered.

"Magic schools," I reply.

No further explanation is necessary, for we have had this debate many a time. From what I understand, four of the seven main schools of magic attract mostly Saroth and three attract mostly Arkonai practitioners. Saroth given access to the Gift become Minders, Shapeshifters, Conjurers, and Destroyers. Conjurers occasionally answer to the title Summoners as well, since most of what they do is call objects and persons from beyond the Veil.

The Arkonai often become Seekers, Healers, or Guardians, whose uncanny reflexes can easily be hidden among the Bereft. The Saroth and Arkonai leaders try to label the schools as either dark or light magic, but if my father has taught me anything, it is that the Seven Gifts simply exist, having no more sense of morality than a newborn baby.

"Ah, I see. Too bad Tellen is not here or we could have a proper argument."

"Over what?" Tellen inquires. "Magic schools again?"

"What else," Katrina confirms, looking amused.

"I just want to go to sleep," I say, not wanting to get into a lengthy discussion.

"So admit you're wrong and leave it at that," Tellen teases. He drops the new firewood near the edge of the existing fire and chooses a small branch to poke at the greedy flames.

Our last debate was over whether or not to keep the fire going throughout the night. Tellen wanted a perpetual fire, I didn't have an opinion, and Katrina didn't think it was wise but finally quit arguing when I observed that most of our enemies could already sense us. I think the winning stroke was Tellen's point that zombies hate fire.

"I'm not wrong," I respond, rising to his bait. "You're proof that I'm not wrong." Annoyance seeps into the statement, and I hope Tellen will pick up on it and back off.

Typical of Tellen, he knows I'm riled, so he presses on.

"I'm special," he says with an easy smile. He settles on the ground next to the fire and continues provoking it until it brightens. "You can argue until the end of time, and I'll keep telling you I'm a Guardian with a few extra toys to play with."

"Lightning is a Destroyer power," Katrina notes. In this debate, she's the neutral one. Since before she could walk, she knew she would become a Shapeshifter. Though most people who don't understand shudder when speaking about dark magic, Katrina is quite comfortable with her abilities. "Perhaps Vic is right that people can cross-train in different schools of magic."

"Then what schools of magic do Vic's powers come from?" Tellen challenges. He directs his gaze to the fire but the question is aimed at Katrina.

"What powers?" I ask with a scoff.

"I do not know," Katrina admits.

"Hey! Still here," I say with a wave. "What powers? I light up when things show up to kill us. Not very impressive if you ask me."

"She really doesn't know," Tellen states to Katrina, sounding amused and baffled. Turning to me, he continues in a serious tone, "Vic, you've got Guardian abilities or something."

"What do you mean 'or something;' do I, or don't I?" I demand. My eyes seek clarification from Katrina, but she's busy glaring at Tellen.

"Do not worry, Vic. We will find answers when we locate your father," Katrina assures me. "We are all tired and cranky. Get some rest."

Predictably, the accusation of being cranky annoys me, but I resist the impulse to throw something at Katrina. Instead, I curl over onto my side—deliberately turning my back on my idiot friends—and try to go to sleep.

My head barely gets down when I fall asleep and have an ultra-weird out of body experience. I can see myself sleeping, but I'm a white orb of light hovering over my own body. I can see in every direction simply by willing it so. I've heard Minders describe their experiences, but nothing in their tales sounds anything like this.

"Do not fear. You are not dead," intones a woman's gentle voice.

As her words touch me, fear I hadn't even recognized slips away. My attention fixes on a figure hovering over our fire. I recognize the woman as my mother, though I've not seen her for more than a decade. A hundred questions crowd my head, but I don't know how to voice them.

My mother smiles sadly and holds forth her hands. "My time is short, Victoria. I bear a message from The Lady. You already know the truth about the world. You will soon make many discoveries and face trials. You are the Chosen Redeemer. Listen to the prophecy, then choose your destiny. Beware betrayal, but do not fear to trust. When all else fails, look within. The Lady will grant you peace at your most desperate hour."

With her speech over, my mother reaches out and touches the glowing white orb that is me. Instantly, I'm awake, cold, and confused. Tellen snores softly from his blanket on the other side of the flickering fire. Katrina's blanket is empty. She must be off on her self-imposed watch duties. I briefly look around, but I'm not surprised when I cannot find her. If I call, she will hear, but I don't want to disturb her meditative watch for something I can't explain.

"Your mother is always with you, Victoria," an ageless female voice says inside my head.

I bite my lower lip to keep from crying out.

"What do you want from me?" I hiss at the voice. "Who are you?" When nothing answers, I mutter, "Great, I'm seeing and hearing things. I can't win."

For reasons I cannot explain, I sense Katrina on the fourth branch up in the tree behind me. Concentrating hard, I know she's in her beetle form and that her attention is methodically considering our tiny camp, having mentally divided it into sections. I call to her silently, but nothing happens. Focusing on her again, I try to see if anything else will be revealed to me, but aside from further conviction that I am correct in everything I've felt about her, nothing changes.

I want to say something profound, but the best I can do is a quiet, "Well, that's … interesting."

Chapter 7:
Breakthrough

The Lady
Combat Arena, Fort Medron

After visiting with Victoria, I turn my attention to the unpleasant task of seeing what manner of ills Jackson Castaloni has uncovered.

Unbidden, the memory of how brilliant a Conjurer Jackson used to be invades my mind. When he was Alec's age, Jackson was entrusted with his first lesson in conjuring inanimate objects. The lesson on drawing bread from the air sparked an obsession.

August Polani repeatedly told Jackson to use the Conjuring Gift with great care, for the ability draws its raw power from the life energies of lesser creatures. Rather than deter the boy, the knowledge intrigued him. Soon, inanimate objects failed to satisfy Jackson's craving for power. Day after day, he pleaded with his master to teach him the advanced arts of summoning creatures from beyond the Veil, deep in the Darklands. When August Polani flatly refused, Jackson stole his collection of ancient texts and fled.

Holding an image of the young Conjurer up beside the ghastly shell of a man that remains, I mourn what was lost. Both the past and present versions of Jackson have a bright spark in their deep green eyes, but whereas the young man's spark indicates excitement, exploration, and discovery, the elder man's spark points to madness.

"Quit standing there, boy!" Jackson snaps at Alec. "I'm ready to begin. Wake the slaves."

The vision of Jackson's former self dissipates as Alec hurries to obey. The child's heart beats frantically with fright, but he channels the nervous energy into carrying out his assignment. Quickly, he makes his way around the tiny dungeon, waking each prisoner. Next, Alec offers each man a cup of water. Finally, he serves them some strips of meat. The task of feeding the three prisoners has the child scrambling back and forth between three of the four walls making up the arena area of this dungeon.

The three captives—well-muscled men—accept the sustenance from the boy's hands. Metal cuffs and chains secure their feet, arms, and waists to the dungeon walls. Their expressions are blank, but otherwise, they appear unharmed, save for ample dirt from whatever travels brought them here and the brand marks of condemned men.

Though tempted to check each man's mind for his name, I refrain for fear that Alec's mind may shut me out should I leave. The child's mind is already defensive. The ease with which Alec moves throughout the sandy pit tells me he has been here many times before. The thought weighs upon me. No child should face such a harsh side of life.

Once finished with his chores, Alec dashes up the stone steps and sits at his uncle's feet.

Jackson nods approval then starts the conjuring ceremony. I ignore the words flowing from Jackson, for the horror of what's happening becomes clearer with each passing second. At first, the prisoners appear weary, but then the weariness threatens their consciousness. One man rallies enough energy to moan a curse at Jackson before slumping against the chains holding him to the wall.

One by one Jackson drains energy from his slaves and channels it into the center of the arena. The sand in the middle begins swirling and shifting color from yellow to gray to black. Next, the circle of sand rises to waist height.

Sensing Jackson's fierce concentration, I consider having Alec interrupt the ceremony, but that would only delay the inevitable, leave me dark to Jackson's purpose, and possibly bring wrath down upon Alec.

The column of swiftly spinning sand rises even higher and swirls faster still. An errant sand grain spins out of the column and catches one prisoner across the cheek, cutting deeply. The room feels alive with energy as the black sand cloud continues spinning violently. As one, the three prisoners jerk against the wall, their chains straining to contain the force holding them upright. A beam of energy escapes and slams into the wall above one prisoner.

As I begin to fear the swirling sand may cut the slaves to pieces, the sand freezes and collapses to the ground. Before the dust cloud can settle, two large gray hands grip the edge of the rift that has been created.

I expect the jerky movements of a zombie's awkward entrance to this world, but instead, the arms smoothly haul their owner out of the rift as quickly as any human. Before I can study the creature, two more join the first. Then, the rift slams shut, sealing these creatures in the natural world.

Nobody moves or speaks for several long heartbeats.

My heart sinks, for I have seen such creatures and the destruction they bring. They are the Denkari, rogue spirit warriors who supported the Outcast's rebellion against Kailon. Though often mistaken as a deity—as am I—the Outcast is simply a diminished immortal. He once held great position and power in the heavens, but he could not be content with himself.

The Denkari possess bodies much like humans, but they are not human. They are taller, stronger, and usually of a hue different than that typical of mankind. Those that possess a color closer to the pink or brown flesh color of a normal human tend to be very pale. They move with the grace and skill Kailon bestowed upon each spirit warrior. Most prefer to wield the ancient spirit swords they were given, but some have shunned these in favor of bows or spirit shards. In the rare event a Denkari is without an actual weapon, he or she can always rely upon retractable claws, poisonous venom, or their unique ability to mentally assail their enemies.

Does Jackson know what he has conjured? The glowing sense of satisfaction swirling about his spirit tells me he knows the Denkari have tremendous power, but I doubt he grasps the full measure of his folly.

The Denkari answer to no man. Only the Outcast can command them. I expect the Denkari to strike down the captives, but they simply stand at the arena's center observing the situation.

"Release the prisoners," Jackson orders Alec. "The creatures will not harm you."

Though scared beyond the ability to speak, Alec does as bid. It takes the boy less than a minute to unlock the shackles binding the three prisoners to the walls.

As the chains fall from the last man's wrists, the three Denkari focus on Alec. In a flash, the lead Denkari plucks Alec up by the neck and slams him against the wall.

A pained yelp from Alec almost disappears beneath Jackson's outraged cry.

"She is here," growls the lead Denkari.

"What are you talking about?" snaps Jackson. "Unhand my apprentice!"

"The Lady of Light," explains the shortest of the Denkari.

Knowing I can no more hide my presence from them than they can from me, I leave Alec and form a ghostly avatar. A spirit shard sheers through the center of my form and shatters against the stone wall, narrowly missing Alec's leg.

"Leave," I say, though I've no delusions they'll actually listen. "This world belongs to Kailon."

"We were invited," chorus the Denkari.

Forcing a smile, I make one last attempt to reason with them.

"You know your master loses in the end, perhaps not now or for a long while yet, but it is inevitable. Why continue this fight? What are these people to you? Why bring destruction upon them?"

"Go choose your champion, Lady. When we slaughter the champion, we will think of you," says the lead Denkari. He follows this with a moderate, almost playful mental blow.

"Forget her. I summoned you. You must obey me." Jackson's voice holds a slight tremor, but he fights for control.

One of the Denkari not holding Alec steps forward and stretches a hand in Jackson's direction. Both cry out in pain as the mental attack fails. The Denkari seem surprised at Jackson's triumph.

After a silent battle of will, the lead Denkari puts Alec down.

"What is it you wish, mortal?"

Grinning, Jackson tries to hide his relief by speaking swiftly.

"Kill these men then come with me. I promised your master an opening, and he promised me a throne. We have plans to make."

Chapter 8:
Unexpected Aid

Katrina Polani
Temporary Camp, Foot of the Karnok Mountains

Something has changed in Vic. I cannot pin down the feeling, but she looks at me differently this morning. I do not wish to give the impression that previously Vic was an empty-headed moron, but there is a spark of knowledge that was not present last night.

Before I can tactfully comment on the change, she bursts forth with the whole saga. "I had a dream last night, a dream of my mother telling me that The Lady has made me the Chosen Redeemer and that I should not fear to trust but I should watch out for betrayal." She proceeds to describe the dream in detail, telling me not only the words but also the scene that unfolded around her. In predictable, straightforward Vic fashion, she ends with a stream of questions. "What prophecy was she talking about? What does it mean? Should I be worried? What's this destiny nonsense? What's the Chosen Redeemer supposed to do anyway?"

Though Tellen is present, Vic's eyes search mine for answers. She must know that I know more than I let on, but how? Once again, I am torn between my father's order to keep silent and my need to level with my young friend.

Oddly enough, Tellen solves my dilemma.

"Don't worry about it, Vic. The legend and prophecy are a kid's story. Your father must have told you the tale long ago and you're remembering it now."

"Tell me, please," Vic orders in a half-pleading tone. She shifts her intense gaze from me to Tellen.

Tellen - Arkonai Huntsman

"We should probably get moving," Tellen says, dragging out the first word. "I'll tell you on the way," he adds as Vic's expression takes on a stubborn cast.

"Tell her while I pack up the camp," I insist. "And do not spare the details." My word to my father said nothing about somebody else telling Vic the prophecy, only that I would not.

The prospect of having no camp breakdown chores puts Tellen in a cheery mood. Sadly, there is not much to do since we escaped Vic's place with very little. I roll the blankets, bury the fire ashes, check each pack, and try to erase any signs of our presence.

If we push hard, we can reach Coldhaven by nightfall, but I am very concerned that we have no food. We do not have much money either, but the villagers will not turn away weary travelers. We should be able to find work in Coldhaven while we decide which direction to pursue. Perhaps someone will know where to find Daniel Saveron.

I half-listen to Tellen's version of the legend containing the prophecy—that may or may not pertain to Vic—to make sure he includes the important points. Frustration mounts in me as Tellen skims over large parts, but thankfully, Vic's astute enough to call him on the vagueness.

"So, you've told me about a goddess who gave a man she loved a pair of magical bracers to save him during the last Great War. Big deal. I've heard the tale before. What's that got to do with a prophecy?" Vic's narrowed eyes are more demanding than her tone. I think she missed her calling to be a bratty princess.

Tellen levels a sympathetic look at Vic.

"If the prophecy's right, the legend bracers *are* yours, Vic." His tone reaches out to ease the revelation.

I almost forgive every annoying thing about Tellen for that gentle tone.

The notion passes when Tellen clears his throat to drive out the traces of sentiment.

"The prophecy says that when the Darkness comes again, the Chosen Redeemer will use the bracers to drive the undead back to the Darklands and destroy the link between the physical and spiritual worlds."

"You mean there may never be walking dead people again?" Vic asks.

A chill runs through me. The idea of a world free of zombies and other Darkland nightmares seems unthinkable.

"So the story says," Tellen replies. He shrugs. "I don't know if it's true, but it's a good story."

For once Vic keeps her thoughts to herself, but I know she believes the prophecy. Her innocent soul has latched on to the hope contained within the legend. I want to caution her that not every sign says the Chosen Redeemer will come soon but that would be a lie. The signs exist. I lose myself in thoughts about what we can expect upon reaching Coldhaven.

Will Vic's father be there? What sort of clue will he leave if he is not there?

Despite my distraction, my instincts are as sharp as ever. Three things happen at once: Vic's eyes light up, Tellen draws his twin daggers, and I turn myself into a dog. Suddenly, a massive wolf stands on the edge of our former camp. Easily a whole head bigger than my dog form and bristling with muscles, the wolf could probably tear us apart without really trying. Despite my fear, I admire the gorgeous blend of white, brown, beige, and black fur. Spotting intelligent, pale blue eyes, it occurs to me that this wolf could be a Shapeshifter, but if he is, he's a master.

I growl and brace for a terrible fight, but nothing happens. The wolf solemnly bows his head, yips once, and bounds away. Something in me reaches out to the wolf. I sense he is a kindred spirit, though I do not understand how I know him. The sense is like feeling part of myself completed. My legs carry me forward a dozen paces before I hear Vic calling me back.

"Wait! He's not a threat! Come look at what he left us!" Vic's voice rings with childlike wonder.

Fighting off the primal instinct to pursue the mysterious wolf, I lope back to Vic and Tellen. Whether friend or foe, I am certain I will see the wolf again.

***

Victoria Saveron
Temporary Camp, Foot of the Karnok Mountains

I have never considered myself blessed by one deity or another, but I must admit that this morning when I noticed we had nothing to speak of in the way of food, I begged The Lady for supplies.

I cannot explain it, but I know this boon comes from her. Father has always warned that the Ancient Ones are not there to fulfill the petty needs of lesser creatures, but in my dream The Lady's agent promised aid at my most desperate hour. Though I hardly count low supplies as my "darkest hour," I figured it couldn't hurt to ask.

Tellen has removed the string binding the bundle together and unfolded the leather sides. Katrina comes back and inspects the gifts brought by the wolf. The contents include three bags for water, three loaves of fresh bread, and three strips of dried meat. Still in dog form, Katrina sniffs carefully at the food.

I throw silent thanks at the departed wolf and wonder if I will ever see him again. He felt familiar, like an acquaintance one recognizes but cannot name. The brief glimpse of him has left a powerful longing in me. Not understanding the feeling, I focus on Katrina who has completed her inspection.

"Is it safe?"

"Only one way to find out," Tellen declares.

Katrina takes on her human form to say, "Wait."

But Tellen has already dropped to his haunches and snatched up a loaf of bread. Before either Katrina or I can act, Tellen takes a huge bite from the bread. The next instant he cries out in agony, drops the bread, clutches his stomach, and collapses.

A scream escapes me. My feet feel like they've turned to stone. I want to go to Tellen but I can't move. Horror and dread have rendered me useless. My heart slams into my throat, choking me with thick sobs that scrape my throat raw. A ringing buzzes in my ears and I think I might faint.

Katrina's eyes widen with shock then narrow with anger.

"Get up, you idiot." She kicks Tellen none too gently in the legs. "That's a terrible thing to do. Vic's about to have an emotional meltdown over there."

Only then do I realize that Tellen's moans have turned into deep, rumbling laughter intermingled with hacking coughs.

Struggling to his feet, Tellen wipes tears from his eyes.

"You should have seen your face, Vic!" He laughs some more, clutching his sides. His breaths come in gasps.

Torn between laughter and the need to punch Tellen, I stare at my friend and try to control my emotions. A small part of me agrees that Tellen played the victim brilliantly, but I still wish Katrina had kicked him harder.

Still chuckling, Tellen picks up one of the two untouched loaves of bread from the leather cloth they lay on and brings it to me.

"Peace offering?" His face twitches as he struggles against more laughter.

"Deal," I reply, closing my eyes and drawing a deep breath as I accept the bread. "But you have to fill the waterbags as penance."

A smile lights up Tellen's face, for he knows he has won a victory.

Katrina turns into a snake long enough to hiss at him then bends down to pick up the last loaf of bread.

"And you get the bread you dropped on the ground."

"It was worth it," Tellen says.

In response, Katrina picks up the three waterbags and tosses them at Tellen. Her expression is unreadable until she turns to tie the rest of the bundle together. Then, I see her faint smile.

"And no fruit," Katrina calls to Tellen as he retreats to carry out his extra chore.

Chapter 9:
Reluctant Redeemer

Victoria Saveron
Path to Coldhaven

When Tellen returns from filling the waterbags, we each heft a pack Katrina has prepared for us and start down the trail leading to Coldhaven, Bright Hope, Coolwater Creek, and eventually the city of Bastion. Though we have not traveled together long, the roles we settle into seem natural. Katrina takes the lead, remaining in her human form to better facilitate carrying her share of the supplies. I stay in the middle, undoubtedly the safest spot for me, and Tellen follows a few steps behind, his hands never more than inches from his daggers.

Dangerous though traveling while distracted can be, I can't shake the dream or Tellen's story. Of course, I had heard the Legend of the Silver Bracers before, though not the version with a prophecy about destroying evil. My father used to tell me the story before tucking me into bed.

Father and I might be reclusive people, but that doesn't mean we're ignorant of the culture around us. I wonder why my father saw fit to omit the prophecy. More than anything, the omission lends credence to the idea of it being true. Father used to tell me that I would, *"know what I need to know when I need the knowledge and not a moment before,"* whenever he didn't feel like explaining something.

Chosen Redeemer.

As the title spins in my mind, I expect a sense of excitement, pride, joy, or eagerness to discover what my future holds. Instead, I feel uncertainty, confusion, and even a slight sense of outrage.

This is a bad idea for many reasons.

Reason one: I'm the last to know anything. This journey of self-discovery may only be days old, but it's slapped me with the realization that my father may not have been as open with me as I previously thought. Father's insistence that I never let anybody know where we live now makes sense. He's always been mysterious.

I used to think our isolation was due to my father's general aversion to people, but his paranoia may have had stronger foundations. Things out to get me because I might become the Chosen Redeemer would explain Father's obsession with weapons readiness and training. There's much about my father that I simply do not know. How can one spend so much time around another person and still feel like a stranger? Does everybody have this problem?

The Redeemers in the legends are always knowledgeable thanks to their close connection with the Lady of Light. Scholars debate whether The Lady is a goddess or merely a servant of Kailon, which means Eternal King. Like the Judges in service to Kailon, the Redeemers were an organization devoted to serving The Lady, but they ceased to exist a few hundred years back. I didn't make the connection before because previously it didn't matter.

Reason two: I'm not a people person. Despite this journey to I-know-not-where with Katrina and Tellen, I have spent much of my life in the cabin either alone or with Father. The rare visits from Shadow were always amusing, but how close can one get to a boy who always wears a black mask and won't even tell you his real name?

The few trips I accompanied Father to Coldhaven or Bright Hope I heeded the orders to keep quiet. A woman from Coolwater Creek used to travel up every fall and winter to teach me how to read, write, and do simple sums, but once I mastered those, Father simply stocked up on books for my continued education.

Reason three: I can't speak very well. As a child, I used to have long conversations with myself or imaginary audiences, but the thought of crowds terrifies me.

When I complained about not having someone to talk to, Katrina appeared more regularly, and when I complained about having only Katrina, Tellen appeared. I'm not complaining about the lack of people, merely stating reasons I'm not comfortable around crowds.

It's not like there's a manual explaining what makes a good Redeemer, but according to Tellen, the Chosen Redeemer will reshape the world. How can one expect to do any world shaping when they get queasy at the thought of public speaking?

Reason four: I am short and slight. Significant height may not be an official hero prerequisite, but it would help command attention. When one starts with as few hero attributes as I do, it's depressing to fall short of the most basic ones.

Maybe I'm being unduly pessimistic, and if that's the case, I may list it as reason four and a half. Redeemers were a cheerful lot if the legends speak truth.

Reason five: I am inexperienced in pretty much everything. Here I lay blame upon my sheltered childhood. Father did his best to raise me not to be a complete brat, but he was away a lot. He always made certain I had plenty of food and knew what to do in case of a zombie attack. We even did drills to that end. I do not view my childhood self as a prisoner. There were never any locks on the cabin door, but there was also nowhere to go and not much to do except play darts, read, cook, clean, or practice sword fighting with a stick from the woodpile.

Reason six: I am not very strong. I do have good stamina thanks to the necessity of walking to fetch drinkable water. I don't even own any weapons, besides the bracers, and they're more like armor than a weapon. I tried to pick up my grandfather's greatsword once and nearly fell over. Like any respectable huntsman, Father taught me tracking, trapping, basic swordplay, and how to handle a bow, but I wouldn't categorize my skills as *expert* in any of these areas.

Reason seven: My life goals are exceptionally moderate. I would like to move to a populated place, perhaps not so populated as Bastion but a place where I can find a decent magic tutor. Self-teaching is definitely not the way to go with magic. Shapeshifters develop different powers as they progress in their training. I'm hoping that means there's a chance I have more useful latent magic abilities than glowing when dangerous things approach. I have a good imagination, but that's not going to impress the undead.

Reason eight: I am not pretty. In every tale ever told, the heroine can at least rely on her looks. It's like these things have a "gawky teenagers need not apply" vibe to them.

Reason nine: I blank out during battles. Tellen and Katrina assure me that whenever the fighting starts I do fine, but I'm pretty sure they're just being kind. One could try to frame it as I am super focused during a battle, but it's scary to think about entering conflict when I've no idea what will happen or how I'll react.

Reason ten: I don't want to save the world. Don't get me wrong, I'd hate for the world to be destroyed. Still, I've no pressing desire to place myself in mortal danger to prevent such a catastrophe.

My father presented the Arkonai worldview of "serve and protect where possible," yet he never demanded I accept the view. I've adopted a simpler "live and let live" philosophy. Katrina's tried to convert me to the Saroth way of thinking, which can be defined as "order through control." I'm not certain what Tellen believes, but the snippets I've gathered tell me he's more in line with the extreme Arkonai view of "meddle in everything."

Even as I finish composing my list of reasons why I would make a terrible Chosen Redeemer I get a faint amused sensation and hear silent words in my mind: *That is why you were chosen.*

"Is something wrong, Vic?" Tellen asks from behind me.

"What?"

In answer, he gently pushes me forward until I stumble along a few more steps.

"You stopped suddenly. Are you all right?"

"Fine," I mumble. My mind fills with conflicting wishes for him to ask more questions and mind his own business. Unconsciously, I stop walking again.

Tellen delivers another nudge in the right direction.

"You're a bad liar, but I'll let it slide because we need to hurry or Katrina will hiss at both of us."

He's right, so I let Tellen herd me toward Coldhaven.

Chapter 10:
Coldhaven's Bargain

The Lady
Gathering Hall, Coldhaven

The old floorboards creak in protest as angry villagers jostle each other for a better position. The Gathering Hall has never seen so many distraught people. The pleas and demands crash into each other, making it very difficult for the two men standing up front to distinguish individual speakers let alone respond.

"Give them what they want!" shouts a youth.

"Get my son back! They took my son!" cries a woman.

"Hold *him* hostage until we get the boy back!" orders a man.

"Why is this happening?" wails a girl.

Elder Willem Baxter holds up both arms in a gesture that begs for calm and, if things continue to deteriorate, could double for a feeble attempt to keep the others at bay.

"Please listen! We will figure out what to do, I promise!"

As it is not good to interfere in the affairs of mortals, I would normally let things proceed as they may, but I sense time passing quickly. I must know their plans if I am to protect my unsuspecting Chosen Redeemer. So, I flood the room with calming emotions until the shouts subside. The effort stretches my ability to interact with the physical world. I would like to know who the dangerous stranger is, but the effort to control the crowd occupies my attention. I don't have the level of intimacy I can have within one mind, but their feelings are clear. People believe the misconception that immortal means all-powerful and all-knowing, but that is simply not true.

The stranger standing a step behind the elder uncrosses his arms and draws even with Coldhaven's leader. A gleam in his eyes dares somebody to give him an excuse for violence.

"We're here to strike a bargain." His words come out slow and even.

"What bargain? What do you want?" demands a woman.

"Three young travelers will arrive soon," says the stranger. "You will welcome them, feed them, and bring them to me at the ruins of Fort Amareth. There you will find the woman and child taken to ensure your cooperation."

"Woman? What woman?" says an old man. "I thought the Chadwick boy was snatched."

"The child will need care when he awakens," the man points out with a cruel smile. "Do I have any volunteers?"

Stunned silence falls over the Gathering Hall.

"I will go," offers the boy's mother.

"No, you will not," hisses her husband.

The stranger considers the woman's statement and shakes his head.

"No, I need somebody … younger … and less wounded."

Confusion crosses the woman's face. In a flash, the man hurls a dagger at the woman. The blade lodges in the muscle just above her left knee. She screams as her stunned husband catches her around the waist and eases her to the ground.

Feeling the husband's anger flare, I focus my calming efforts on keeping him from giving the man an excuse for murder. An outraged murmur ripples through the crowd as my efforts shift away from them, but I do not expect trouble from anybody else, save maybe the outspoken youth.

With a thought, the stranger recalls the dagger and wipes the blood on the stunned elder's sleeve. A few deft flicks of the dagger remove the rest of the billowy, white sleeve. Calmly, the man bundles the sleeve into a ball and throws it at the woman's husband before returning his dagger to the sheath.

"Bind that wound," the stranger orders. To the woman, he adds, "It will heal in a few days, but I'm afraid the walk to Fort Amareth would be too strenuous for you."

"If you want the travelers so badly, why don't you capture them yourself?" asks the woman. Her voice is soft and strained with pain. She speaks simply so she won't think about her leg. Relief and guilt flicker in her eyes as tears stream down her face.

"Yes, why involve others?" inquires Elder Baxter. He glances down at his bare arm, frowning at the ruins of his shirt. "We are no threat to you. Even if we wanted to interfere, we couldn't."

"They're cowards," mumbles the bitter young man. "The travelers are probably great warriors he's afraid to fight."

The stranger smiles languidly, blinks slowly, and then springs forward, seizes the challenger, throws him to the ground, and places a boot on his neck.

The crowd recoils as those in the front put their backs into gaining distance from the demonstration.

"Never start something you can't finish, kid," advises the man. He presses down on the boy's throat hard enough to cut off the air supply. Then, he returns to Elder Baxter's side as if nothing has happened.

The young man slowly sits up and rubs his throat.

"Who are they?" His question is curious but defiant.

"That is none of your concern," replies the man. Raising his eyes to the crowd, the stranger adds, "Think about how you will obtain my prizes."

"Why should we help you?" calls a man from the back.

Shouts of agreement and disapproval ring out. Regardless of opinion, people back away from the man as quickly as possible in case the stranger decides another object lesson is in order.

"What's in it for us?" presses the new man. A shove sends him stumbling forward and another pocket forms around him.

"I'm glad you asked. If you hadn't spoken, I might have forgotten to mention that one of my men wishes to open a Darkland portal here in Coldhaven." The stranger raises his hands to quell the cries of dismay. "However, if you fulfill your side of this simple bargain, I will convince him to move on to another village."

Shifting my focus to ascertain whether or not the man speaks truth, I sense only calm. The man might be lying, but if so, he believes the lie. He may yet be deceived, but I cannot dwell on alternate scenarios right now. I need to concentrate. My distraction allows the crowd to rumble with negative emotions.

"You'll kill us!" wails a woman.

"We should kill you right now," mutters the angry young man.

Thankfully, the violent stranger does not hear him.

"We should do it," says the man standing alone in the middle.

His statement stuns the others into silence. "What've we got to lose? We capture the travelers, turn 'em over, perhaps even earn a fee, and go on about our business. The Chadwick lad gets returned and things end well. There are happy endings all around." As he speaks, he turns in a slow circle, making eye contact with his neighbors.

"Things will *not* be well." The speaker, a young woman I am familiar with, confronts the collaborator. "This is murder ye'd have us plotting, Ederon. Oy, think of The Lady, bless her name and gentle spirit. What would she say if she could see us?" She glares at those gathered around, shaming most into lowering their gazes.

Sara Andari might have felt my presence if emotions had not been running so high. I know her, for she seeks to know the One I serve. For a fraction of a second, I wish I could have kept her silent, for I know what is coming, but as usual, mortals make their own decisions and must stand by them. Instead of focusing on regret, I channel abiding peace and let her know I am proud she spoke up.

Catching the stranger's gaze and responding to a silent order, Ederon places a firm hand on the girl's left shoulder.

"You should have stayed out of it, Sara." With that, he spins her around and wrenches her right arm up behind her back. Then, he marches her through the crowd and shoves her toward the stranger.

Easing Sara to a kneeling position, the stranger speaks with mock sincerity.

"Thank you for volunteering. You seem like a pillar of this community." He draws his dagger and taps it on her shoulder as if he would knight her. "I think they'll come through for you. What say you? Have we changed your mind about the travelers?"

"It's still wrong," Sara whispers.

"I'll take that as a 'not yet,' but give the idea time, my dear. I'm sure you'll come around."

Nobody interferes with Ederon and the stranger as they guide Sara out of the Gathering Hall.

Chapter 11:
Shadow's Choice

The Lady
Path to Coldhaven

The conflict raging within Shadow causes his spirit to shine like a hillside fire on a moonless night. Having witnessed the scene in the Gathering Hall, Shadow knows his job got a whole lot harder. Few deny Huntmaster Oren's success rate, but many disapprove of his methods. Shadow's reluctance to fulfill the contract has grown to a deep conviction that doing so would be wrong, yet Oren's threats cannot simply be dismissed.

These facts, I gather from Shadow's body language and surface thoughts. Much of him still lies beyond my reach. He has no wish to defy his father by breaking the contract, but he cannot help the feeling that Victoria's uncle should be denied the bracers.

"What would Dina do?" Shadow whispers to the night air.

Upon hearing the name a dozen small puzzles resolve for me. Shadow keeps his mind locked tightly, but this name helps me breach his defenses. Inside his mind, a thousand scenes flash, some good, some regrettable. The storm of emotions whirls around the edges of Shadow's consciousness, but deeper in, a different sort of battle takes place.

Knowing the time to reveal myself has come, I access Shadow's mind and appear before him, holding my hands out in a calming gesture.

The light surrounding my body catches his attention without destroying his vision. He slams his eyes shut, but the image is already burned onto his brain, letting me dispense with the avatar.

Talking here should be safe, but with the increase in Darkland creatures, I have no wish to distract Shadow for long. Winning a convert does me no good if he dies.

In the long run, I believe a swift end is sometimes kinder, but such debates must wait. Victoria's party approaches. Shadow's internal conflict must be resolved now.

"You have been 'Shadow' a long time. Choose a side, Devin. People believe there are only two sides, light and dark, but you and I know that there is a third choice: the shadows. Before this moment, you have chosen based on instinct. You are a great hunter and warrior, but you have no real cause. That is why fighting often felt wrong. I have a cause for you. Will you hear it?"

"What cause?" Shadow asks. His voice sounds brittle like it has gone unused for ages.

"The one who approaches will one day become my Chosen Redeemer." I send him an image of Victoria and her companions.

Shadow's mind sharpens.

"Vic?"

I nod.

"I have set her apart, but she must not stand alone. Others should prepare the way. Warn her of Oren's trap."

"And if she ignores my warning? What then?" He struggles to keep his voice low.

"She will likely ignore your warning," I reply. "That does not change the fact that she should make a conscious decision." I believe Victoria will go to Coldhaven anyway. This warning has more to do with Shadow than Victoria.

"That makes no sense," Shadow mutters. "If you want me to save her, I should stop her from reaching Coldhaven or fulfill my contract."

"The choice is yours, Devin, but you must make it now." Saying thus, I leave his mind.

***

Victoria Saveron
Path to Coldhaven
"Halt!" calls a figure standing in the middle of the path.

"Does that ever work?" Katrina wonders. She clutches the walking staff she picked up when we stopped for lunch hours ago. She slows her approach but does not stop. Her body language tells me she's

53

tense, but if she truly expected a fight, she would already have assumed her snake or dog form.

"Who are you?" I try to keep things cordial, but my voice snaps anyway. My aching feet don't feel up to running, and the pack that seemed light this morning feels like a mountain across my shoulders. I'm in no mood for a fight, but this person stands between me and a good night's rest. My brain's too tired to figure out if it's a man or a woman, but I'm reasonably certain the figure is no zombie.

"I am called Shadow, and I bear a message from The Lady."

My Shadow? My mind reels.

"Shadow as in 'Huntsman Shadow,' son of Supreme Huntmaster Lekros?" asks Tellen.

"The same," confirms the figure.

"Show us," I challenge, speaking softly to steady my voice.

Tellen and Katrina shoot me confused glances, but Shadow knows what I am talking about. Nodding, he tugs at a string tucked under his shirt and pulls forth a pendant. Whispering, he makes the pendant light up. It glows with the same eerie yellow light I remember from childhood. For a moment, I think I may finally see my friend's face, but those hopes dash as the light disappears into the black cloth mask obscuring his features.

"All right, point proven. State your message and be on your way," orders Katrina.

"Do not stop in Coldhaven. It is a trap."

"How would you know that?" questions Katrina. "Perhaps this is the trap."

"Shadow wouldn't do that," I declare, putting more confidence into my tone than I feel. The child I knew would never harm me, but how much of that boy is left in this man?

"No huntsman would," Tellen confirms. "Trickery is a Saroth thing."

Shadow mumbles something in an old, barely used version of the Arkonai language, but it is too soft to hear over Katrina's retort.

"The Arkonai I have known are plenty fond of traps."

Tellen's ears pick up Shadow's statement, causing him to become very still.

"What did you say?" I ask Shadow.

The answer comes from Tellen.

"We may have a problem."

"What now?" I'm thoroughly tired of bad news.

"Why?" demands Katrina a split-second later.

"What awaits us in Coldhaven has been set in motion by Oren. People call him 'Destroyer,'" Tellen explains.

"*People call him 'Destroyer.'*"

~Tellen

His words chill me. I have never met Huntmaster Oren, but I must press on into the village if I want to ask about my father. It might be the first brave thing I've ever intended to do, and it leaves me nauseous with fear. Nevertheless, I'm drawn to the welcoming lights of Coldhaven like a moth to flame.

"We're still going," I declare.

"Very well, but we must be vigilant," Katrina warns.

"If I die, I'm blaming you," Tellen says. He means to lighten the mood, but the words stick in my heart like an arrow.

"Go with The Lady's blessing." Shadow bows to us and slips away.

Before we cover half the remaining distance to Coldhaven, the great wolf who gave us the food appears in the middle of the path. Eyeing us balefully, the wolf lowers his head and growls. Then, he bounds off into the trees lining the path. A few more yips come at us from the tree line.

"He wants us to follow him," Katrina notes.

"That's our second warning away from this place, we should probably heed it," Tellen points out.

My heart sinks. Now I am torn in two directions. Strong feelings bid me to follow the wolf to safety and to face whatever awaits us in the village.

"Go if you must. I must find my father. Thank you for your aid. I can make it from here."

"We're not leaving you," snaps Katrina.

Tellen sighs and moves ahead of us.

"Knowing Oren, there's probably an elaborate trap waiting. If we're going step into it, we might as well do it sooner rather than later. I'm cold and hungry." Adjusting his pack, he mutters, "They'd better feed us before trying to kill us."

Chapter 12:
Collaborators and Captives

The Lady
Path to Coldhaven

Soon after Shadow leaves in one direction and Vic, Tellen, and Katrina continue toward Coldhaven, I sense the lone figure hiding beneath the brush alongside the path. I might not have even picked up on his presence had Shadow not nearly stepped on the man. The slight feeling of alarm and the subsequent rush of relief catch my attention.

Focusing on the man, I realize he is Ederon, Oren's new lackey. As soon as he thinks it is safe, Ederon rises and scampers back to his master. To save myself the trouble of following the slippery spy through the forest's twists and turns I simply place a mental marker within Ederon's mind so I can find him when he stops.

I can, of course, split my attention quite well, but instinct tells me Ederon's message will alter Oren's plans, which will in turn affect Victoria and the people of Coldhaven. The rapid pace Ederon sets tells me Oren's camp cannot be far. While I wait, I check on Victoria's progress. By the time she and her friends safely reach the first house, Ederon has also arrived at his destination.

The camp Ederon unwittingly leads me to consists of a modest fire tended by two bored men, two trussed up captives, and a single tent from which I sense Oren. A quick search of the guards' minds reveals their names and brief glimpses into their dispositions.

As soon as I see the camp, I understand why Oren chose not to attack Victoria directly. She may not understand her abilities, but they would be more than a match for this crew. Markesh McArn, a Bereft with an obsession for Saroth conjuring magic, has devoted his life to preserving their knowledge. Lerik, Oren's unofficial apprentice, is more a loyal servant than an able fighting companion. Had Oren's orders simply been to kill Victoria, he would not have bothered with the other two, but the man knows his business, including when to outsource certain tasks.

"Well, look at what the night spat back," Lerik notes.

"It's the disgruntled farmer," says Markesh. "Welcome back. Pull up a log and we can have us a good chat. These two ain't much for conversation." He gestures at the two captives slumped against each other, sound asleep.

"I need to speak with Oren," Ederon says.

"Why are you back?" asks Oren, emerging from his tent. "I told you to watch for the girl."

"I did. She's probably arriving at the village as we speak, but it won't work I tell ya. Some fella calling himself Shadow already warned her it was a trap."

"Why's the girl still going to the village if this Shadow fellow done warned her?" wonders Markesh.

"Don't question the good fortune, Markesh," scolds Lerik.

"What exactly did Shadow tell the girl?" Oren asks, ignoring the underlings.

Ederon dutifully repeats what he can remember of the conversation. Though it is far from a perfect rendition, he manages to get the main points across.

"The girl still has no idea what the trap is exactly, but—"

"That's all right. *We* still got no idea what the trap is exactly," Markesh pipes up.

"What do we do now? I doubt the lass will stay long enough to hear them out." Ederon looks curious to hear the answer.

Oren stares into the fire for a long moment before replying.

"We make this a more open trade instead of a trap." Pointing to the prisoners, he adds, "Get them up. We're paying the villagers a visit."

"Can I bring my friends?" asks Markesh, climbing to his feet.

"Of course, we may need them," Oren answers, "just remember, no summoning without my permission. Understand?"

Markesh smiles brightly and nods.

***

Victoria Saveron

Home of Elder Willem Baxter, Coldhaven

For people waiting for the right moment to attack us, the folks in Coldhaven sure are a friendly lot. As we near the first house, a group of children meet us and escort us to the Gathering Hall, but before we can settle in, Elder Willem Baxter and his wife, Mary, whisk us off to their home for a hot meal.

Even as we leave the Gathering Hall, I notice our young guides are nowhere to be found. I'm guessing that they're already alerting the rest of the village to our presence, and I'm starting to wonder if I have a death wish. What part of *trap* didn't sink in the first time?

The villagers' cheerful smiles give me chills, and Katrina eyes everybody suspiciously. Only Tellen seems genuinely relaxed. He's up ahead with Mary Baxter, chatting away like he hasn't a care in the world. Every few seconds I'm quelling another intense urge to drop the pack I'm carrying and run out of Coldhaven.

Oddly enough, the meal turns out to be a rather pleasant affair. Once I'm sure the food has not been poisoned, I dig into the generous supply of hot bread and warm, filling chicken and dumpling soup. By silent agreement, both sides keep the conversation off the main issue. We trade stories about zombie attacks, harvesting and hunting woes, and guesses at how many snowfalls we'll have this winter. Tellen tells our hosts some of his more amusing hunting adventures, and time passes.

Sometime during dessert, I realize the desire to know the problems facing these people has completely deserted me.

Before consciously making any plans, I find myself on my feet with every eye upon me. Manners kick in quickly and I speak.

"Thank you for the wonderful meal, but we should be leaving now."

Tellen and Katrina also rise, followed quickly by our hosts.

"You can't leave!" exclaims Willem Baxter.

"Please do not go," says Mary Baxter. "We would love for you to stay the evening. We have so much to talk about." Her voice maintains a gentle, slightly rapid cadence, but her smile fails to erase the worry from her eyes.

When did I gain the ability to read people's eyes? I check again to be sure and get the same impression. Whatever's going on in this creepy little village, this woman thinks my leaving would be horrible. I search my brain for a suitable way to get to the heart of the matter, when as usual Katrina takes care of it.

"All right, I have had enough of the pleasantries," declares Katrina. "Let's skip to the point. What happened? Who or what's been threatened and what does it have to do with us?"

"I have no idea what you're talking about, dear one. We simply insist you stay for the night. It's far too cold to sleep comfortably out of doors, and we—"

"Oh, it's no use, Mary!" cries Willem, sitting down in his chair. He looks relieved after the outburst. "It's obvious they know something's going on. We're simply no good at this sort of thing."

"So state your case and let us make a decision," Katrina prompts.

"Two of our own have been taken by a man claiming he'll trade 'em fair for you lot," explains the elder.

Tellen's hands hover near his daggers, but his eyes gaze mournfully at the last two bites of pie he didn't finish.

"Such a shame."

I'm going to give him the benefit of the doubt and assume he's referring to the missing villagers.

"Aye, but there's more," states the elder, suddenly looking older. "If we fail to go through with the trade, the man says he'll have a Darkland portal opened right here. If that happens we'll be lucky to escape with our lives."

"This is the hardest thing we've ever faced," Mary Baxter whispers, "but what can we do?"

"We could stay and fight them," I offer, though I know that plan is flawed.

"How do you even know we're the 'lot' the man's after?" Tellen queries.

"We were told to expect three young travelers," Mary explains. "There are few enough travelers in Coldhaven this time of year. He must have meant you. Will you help us?"

"No," Katrina and Tellen say simultaneously. Katrina's tone is matter of fact, and Tellen's voice contains only a hint of uncertainty.

"Yes," I answer. I meant to say *no*, but somehow it didn't work out that way.

Tears spring to Mary's eyes. Before I can move, I'm gasping for breath thanks to a crushing embrace.

"Oh, you dear, dear, sweet child. You don't know what this means to us. I knew you would help! I just knew it!"

After an old woman anoints you with tears and thanks, backing out on your word feels very wrong.

"I will help, but I cannot speak for my friends," I say, before Katrina or Tellen can protest.

"That's not happening," declares a new voice. The man sounds nervous yet determined. "I want my daughter back."

For a split-second, I think the voice belongs to my father, but I'm quickly disappointed. As one, my friends and I spin to face the newcomer.

I don't remember what happened next, but soon, I become aware of Mary Baxter bashing a wooden spoon against a metal bucket and screaming.

"Stop it! Stop it! This isn't helping!"

Instinctively, I freeze and find myself in the common room surrounded by six men moaning and clutching various injuries. Katrina's in her snake form in one corner hissing at two men carrying sharpened sticks.

Tellen has one dagger tucked under Willem Baxter's neck and another warding off a man whose expression says he wishes to be elsewhere.

"Get out of here, Vic," Tellen barks.

Katrina's cold glare contains the same message.

"No, Victoria, please stay," orders yet another new male voice. "I insist."

A small, frightened gasp from Mary Baxter freezes my blood. Three futures—and their prices—play out in my mind. I do not know how I know what I know, but the knowledge comes as naturally as watching a hundred sunsets and then one day truly understanding the magnificence contained therein.

At the risk of sounding mad, I will simply say that these thoughts are mine, yet they do not come from me. My friends and I can escape if we flee immediately, but that path demands the sacrifice of Coldhaven's people. We can fight and perhaps prevail, condemning only ourselves, the villagers in this room, and the two hostages. The only path leading to life is the one that makes the least sense: surrender.

Slowly, the village men littered around me pick themselves off the ground and stand to either side of the leader, who must be Oren. Likewise, the two men who had attacked Katrina and the one being held back by Tellen's dagger retreat.

Once the new battle lines have been established, I speak in a voice I hardly recognize.

"Let Tellen and Katrina go in peace." I sound way too calm. "They must walk a different path."

"Done," Huntmaster Oren agrees.

He lies.

I know he lies, and he knows I know he lies. Still, we will both pretend he speaks truth. I smile like I have earned a great concession, for I also know that he will keep Tellen and Katrina away from me to give the people of Coldhaven the impression he still has honor. Their belief has bought him obedience. When that illusion shatters, they will rise up against him. The knowledge burns like physical pain in my chest, but I cannot speak of it. The time is not yet right.

"Have your pets stand down," Oren orders.

Katrina hisses in response.

"Let me speak with them," I say.

"No." Looking triumphant, Huntmaster Oren turns to Katrina. "You, Saroth, take on your human form and stay in it or I will kill this woman."

Mary whimpers as Oren's blade pricks the sensitive skin on her neck.

Once Katrina obeys, Oren addresses Tellen.

"Let the good elder go, boy."

Tellen looks like he wants to fill the room with lightning. I know he can, but the results would be disastrous. The air thickens and crackles with energy as Tellen draws on his powers.

Swallowing a painful lump, I plead with my friend.

"Do as he says, Tellen." I stare hard into his eyes, hoping he'll read the rest of my message: *Wait. There will be another time to fight.*

Straining to break through Tellen's stubbornness, I accidentally sense a young woman and a boy waiting by the front door.

Recognizing the signs of Tellen accessing his gifts, Oren breathes more threats.

"My contract is for Victoria. It stipulates only that she be alive upon delivery. If you release so much as a spark, I will hurt her, kill the Saroth girl, and beat you to within inches of the Veil's gates beside."

For an eternal second Tellen simply stares back at me, ignoring Oren, but finally, he straightens and sheaths his daggers.

"What happens now?" asks the nervous elder.

"Now, Victoria allows my men to—"

"First release the captives waiting outside," I interrupt.

"They're here?" asks one of the village men, sounding stunned.

Oren's eyes widen with surprise then narrow with anger. He nods curtly and dispatches one of the men to retrieve the other captives.

"Release the boy," Oren orders when the errand is done.

The young woman's father realizes the order's implications almost before I do.

"What about my daughter? I demand—"

"You do not get to make demands. You are at my mercy," Oren informs the man. He makes eye contact with each of the village men and continues speaking. "Victoria has bargained for her friends, and as a gesture of good will, I am releasing the child. I will keep Sara until we reach our destination to keep my contract in line and purchase your cooperation. You will keep Victoria's friends here until I send Sara back. If I see them again, she will die. Do you understand?"

One by one, the village men nod. Then, with permission from Oren, one of the villagers scrambles to release the boy. A happy reunion takes place, and the ropes that previously bound the child are thrown at Tellen's feet.

"Bind Victoria's hands together in front of her, slave travel style," Oren instructs. "Secure her ankles too, but be sure she can still walk."

Though Oren deeply wishes it, I do not react to his statement. Slave travel style is a humiliating way to truss a prisoner. It involves wrapping rope around one's midsection and securing each elbow to that. Then, the wrists are bound together and attached by a short length to yet another cord that wraps around the person's neck. A final system of ropes provides leads which can be used to guide a prisoner about or hobble them like a beast of burden. Depending on how one arranges the ropes, the prisoner can be made to appear in a constant state of supplication.

"Stop it." Katrina does not raise her voice, but her words carry as much weight as Oren's.

Though I do not remember moving, my bracers fill the room with blinding light and I'm in front of Katrina with one of Oren's throwing daggers in each hand. The light fades quickly, but every eye remains dazzled for a few moments.

Had the daggers hit their target, they would have only grazed Katrina, but they carry Oren's point: *do not interfere*. Since I intercepted them, I too made a point: *my surrender cannot be forced, only offered*. To further emphasize my point, I kneel, place both daggers—heel forward—on the ground and slide them toward Oren.

The move causes a murmur to rise from the village men. Mary Baxter starts muttering prayers under her breath. Both Oren and I know the balance of power has shifted. He knows he must conclude this soon or the people of Coldhaven will awaken from their fear-induced stupor.

"Now, boy," Oren growls.

"Do not do this, Vic," Katrina urges. "We need you." She places a hand on my right shoulder and squeezes hard, yet another plea to come to my senses.

I'm touched by the tender, broken tone with which my friend speaks. Reaching up with my left hand, I grip her wrist.

"It will not be for long," I promise.

Tellen scoops up the various lengths of rope and approaches, kneeling before me.

"Remove her gloves first, and remember I will check your work," Oren warns.

"I'm sorry, Vic," Tellen says, reaching to bind my hands.

Chapter 13:
Breakout

Katrina Polani
Storage room of the Gathering Hall, Coldhaven
"You make a lousy prisoner," Tellen teases. "Relax." To emphasize his point, he crosses his ankles, tucks interlaced fingers behind his head, shuts his eyes, and leans back against the wall next to the door. Despite his words and carefree tone, Tellen bears the watchfulness of a patient huntsman waiting for prey to approach. I'm not certain how Arkonai huntsmen sense the world around them, but I suppose it's akin to my ability to feel the surroundings better in snake form than any other.

In dog form, I pace the small room the foolish militia members left us in. Though the room lacks windows and has only one door, its designers had not meant it to hold any captives let alone ones with magical abilities. The crack along the bottom of the door offers one escape route, and several breaks along the foundation offer a few more. A mouse has even left a convenient hole leading to the main room. I could be out of here in seconds. My concern is not in actually escaping; rather it has everything to do with the step after that.

Halting my pacing, I cock my ears to listen. The men's voices, which would have registered as low rumbles to my human ears, echo loudly in my skull. Even if they're not speaking, I hear their restless movements and rough breathing.

Freeing Tellen must be my first priority, but it will not be easy. In addition to the six militiamen, Oren left one of his personal lackeys to oversee our imprisonment. After a moment's calculation, I determine that two village men stand just outside the door to this storage room. The other four huddle near the fire and the man called Markesh paces across the front of the room, arguing quietly with himself. One guard I could handle, perhaps two or three, but seven guards would be able to overwhelm me before I can secure Tellen's release.

If I cannot beat them in a fair fight, I will have to fight unfairly.

"As soon as they come to collect us, we can jump them and make our escape," Tellen announces cheerfully. He closes his eyes and draws in deep, relaxing breaths.

Having gained what I could from the heightened senses of my dog form and tired of the pungent odor of unwashed bodies, I return to my human form and take two steps forward to quietly share my findings with Tellen.

"Welcome back," Tellen greets, opening his eyes.

"How did you know I had changed forms?"

"Your tread changed," he replies. Reaching up with both arms for a good stretch, Tellen yawns then lets his hands drop to the ground. "So, what's the plan? It can't be any crazier than my plan?"

"What's your plan? And what makes you think I have one?" I challenge, though a plan begins to sprout in my mind.

"To answer your second question, I don't know," Tellen admits with a shrug. He climbs to his feet and glances at the door to make sure nothing has come through it in the second he was distracted. "Something's changed. You're … calmer … and deadlier."

"And to answer my first question?"

"I still have the baydonberries," he reminds, patting the small pouch attached to a belt loop in his pants, "and you still have that Saroth fire you can conjure in a pinch."

"Forget it. We do not know how powerful those corrupt berries will be. The explosion would as likely kill us as break us free."

"I knew you wouldn't like it," Tellen concedes, "so tell me your better, saner, safer plan for busting out of here."

Clamping down on annoyance, I explain what I know.

"There are seven men out there, including Markesh. They are spread throughout the room. I cannot win such a fight alone, so I need to draw them in here where you can help."

"How are you going to get them back here?"

"I shall go out into the main room long enough to show myself, retrieve an item if necessary, and retreat back here," I say, wishing it could work that smoothly. "Then, we go with your original plan to simply attack them when they enter."

"What item?" Tellen asks, picking up on the hesitation in my tone. His dubious expression tells me what he thinks of the plan. "Am I going to disapprove of this unnamed item?"

"Probably."

Narrowing his keen brown eyes, Tellen searches my face for answers.

"Wait. You're not talking about Markesh's Conjuring scroll, are you? We don't even know what's on it!"

"Neither do the guards," I point out, trying to hide the fact that I am impressed he spotted the scroll. "Markesh is out there right now, dying to use that scroll. I say we give him the chance, but if he is unwilling to unleash whatever the scroll binds, I can do it." I do not even bother trying to hide a wicked grin. "It would be quite the distraction."

Holding out his palms in a halting motion, Tellen asks, "Have you thought about what happens after we release whatever is on that scroll?"

"We can worry about that after dealing with the guards," I say, aware that the edge of my voice has sharpened.

Dropping his hands and ducking his chin, Tellen closes his eyes, as if praying to The Lady for wisdom. When he looks up, his earnest eyes demand my attention.

"We can't kill them, Katrina. The people of Coldhaven aren't evil. They're scared."

Sudden rage grips me, pounding through my head like martial drums. The memory of Tellen binding Vic's hands for Oren fills me with a lust for revenge, but just as quickly, the emotion leaks away as reason prevails. Much as I wish to blame Tellen, he had no choice but to carry out the order. Defiance would only have earned somebody— likely me—an early grave. Oren's order to Tellen was nothing more than to prove the extent of our powerlessness. I silently curse the Arkonai and their need to exert power over each other and everybody else in the world. My people can be just as cruel, but at least they tend to do their own dirty work.

Trying to cling to the fading scraps of my anger, I ask, "What about Vic?"

"What about her?"

As the anger continues retreating, a cool sense of helplessness rushes to take its place.

"We have to get out so we can help her," I insist, loathing the new emotion.

"I want to help Vic as much as you do, but we can't do it by killing innocents!" Tellen's voice vibrates with the force of his convictions.

That gets a bitter laugh from me.

"None of them are innocent."

"That may be, but we still need a plan," Tellen gently reminds me. Tentatively, he grips my shoulders. "This is bigger than the people of Coldhaven, and it's bigger than us. I agree we need to get out of here and help Vic, but we'll need the villagers' help to get to Fort Amareth without Oren knowing." We'd picked up that little detail from the loose-lipped village men who herded us into this pathetic prison.

"We should steal supplies." Though not a serious suggestion, I am frustrated enough to bring it up to bother Tellen.

"We could steal supplies, but not cooperation," Tellen explains. "I don't know this area well enough to guide us to the fort before Oren, but somebody here should have that knowledge. We need a guide, or at least a map."

"So what would you—"

Surprised and frightened shouts and curses from the main room drive the rest of the thought from my mind. A crash and defiant screams join the continued frantic shouts and the thunderous roar of boots slamming down on wood. I exchange a quick, questioning look with Tellen. He seems grim but resigned.

Nodding toward the other room, he folds his arms over his chest, and says, "Try not to permanently damage anyone."

Diving toward the mouse hole and praying not to meet the mouse, I take on my beetle form and scramble through.

"And don't forget to let me out!" Tellen calls after me.

The scene that meets my eyes is one of pure chaos, and I realize that our disagreement over releasing the creatures bound to the scroll has become moot. Markesh stands atop a wooden chair reading from his scroll. Three zombies stumble around the room, disoriented by the ample light. Their moans and grunts provide an oddly fitting counterpoint to the men's crazed cries.

After wasting several seconds trying to locate the man with the key to the storage room, I notice a fourth zombie and decide Tellen's going to have to wait. The scroll likely only carries one or two more zombies as binding more than five to one parchment can be very difficult, but the room seems plenty full right now.

"Die, foul creatures!" one of the village men screams. "Return to the Darklands, Outcast's spawn!"

Most of the other men keep their comments to simple curses.

Taking on my dog form, I weave through the struggling figures. Without giving Markesh time to think, I bark once, leap, and catch the scroll in my mouth, jerking my head violently several times to yank it from his grasp. Then, ignoring his anguished screams, I use my paws and teeth to rip the scroll to shreds. The paper smells deliciously musky, but before I can sample it, Markesh's boot comes crashing down from above.

Twisting my body away from the boot, I bump into a zombie who grunts in protest. Inspiration strikes and I let loose a series of menacing barks, using my body and well-timed nips to herd the zombies toward Tellen's prison. Once backed into the corner, the zombies pound on the door, eager to escape the almighty racket raised by me and the angry men.

While my unwitting help tears at the door, I keep up a steady racket to spur them on and run back and forth behind them to prevent a retreat. Spotting the belt with Tellen's daggers, I race over to retrieve them, leaping high and snatching them much the same as I had the scroll. As I land with the prize, Markesh appears and kicks me squarely in the side, forcing me to drop the belt with the daggers.

My pained yelp turns into a human sound as I undergo the change and roll forward simultaneously. Pulling out one of Tellen's daggers, I slash at Markesh's left boot. The sharp blade slices through the thick leather and cuts into the leg beneath, earning a chilling noise from Markesh. Before he can recover, I jam the dagger back into its sheath, turn back into my canine form, gather the belt with my teeth, and race to deliver the weapons to Tellen.

Sprinting past dumbfounded men, I arrive as the zombies break through the door. Changing to snake form, I whip my tail around the nearest zombie's leg and yank hard. As expected, the limb comes off with a wet-sounding pop. Suppressing the urge to shudder, I toss the limb in the general direction of the men trying to contain the zombies. Shrieking, they scatter.

The legless zombie leans hard against his fellows, widening the gap. Turning back to dog form, I trot through and present my prize to Tellen.

"Took you long enough," he grouses. His grin contradicts the words as he straps the belt around his waist and draws the daggers. "I'll forgive the dog spit this time. Let's finish this."

Four unmistakable sounds of arrows striking flesh combine with zombie death cries to demand our attention. Their bodies flop to the ground and turn to dust that mingles with the splinters from the door's remains.

Tellen drops into a defensive stance.

I crouch low, ready for anything that comes through that door, except the person who actually strolls in.

"What are you standing there for?" demands Shadow. "Let's go. We have a couple of damsels in distress to rescue."

"Call Vic a damsel in distress to her face," Tellen dares, following Shadow into the main room. "I want to see what she does."

Chapter 14:
Battle for Coldhaven

Katrina Polani
Streets of Coldhaven, just outside the Gathering Hall
Dog form can do well for melee fights against a reasonable number of ordinary foes, and snake form has proven quite effective against zombies. Still, at times such as this, I wish I could use a weapon like Shadow's bow which is currently out, arrow nocked, but not quite pointed at a specific target. Though I have recreationally used a bow, I would be useless with one in a real battle.

As expected, Tellen keeps his daggers at the ready. Someday I hope to be able to wield a dagger or short sword as it would greatly increase the combat effectiveness of my human form. Unfortunately, my transformation skill level lies far below that necessary to affect a weapon. Any Shapeshifter apprentice can weave their clothes into their transformations, but only masters can incorporate additional objects into their creature forms.

Legends speak of Shapeshifters, such as Kian the Conqueror, who could take the form of a dragon and absorb the dust of former zombies to make his fire especially toxic to humans. Modern tales might be more modest, but I am proud to say my great-grandmother, Ilianna Caresh, is among those spoken about in awed whispers. She used to carry a sturdy oak branch and distribute the specks making up the branch into a thin, yet durable, shell whenever she would take to panther form.

I stay in my human form, but I am prepared to switch if necessary. I have a decent reputation for transformation speed, but

71

each of my forms come up short in this situation.

A semicircle consisting of nearly every citizen of Coldhaven has formed around us. Most of the men clutch torches which cast the crowd in an eerie light. Some of the men carry hunting bows, and half a dozen more clutch swords. For a while only faint shuffles and murmurs reach across the twenty or so feet of empty space between us. I scan the assembly and try to determine who might pose the greatest threat, but much of what I encounter in their expressions is fear, not threat.

"Stand aside," orders Shadow. "We have business elsewhere."

Several people respond.

"We need you," says a child.

"Stay and help us!" begs a woman.

"We come to ask ya to take up our cause," explains a man.

Tellen whistles sharply and waves for silence.

"Why should we help you?" I demand, seizing the opening provided by the sudden quiet.

"How can we help?" asks Shadow, keeping his voice neutral. "We haven't time to hear everybody out so I'll ask the elder to summarize for us."

"There's no time!" protests a man.

"They're coming!" warns a woman, her voice high with panic.

Straightening from his ready stance, Shadow makes his weapons disappear. I had seen Tellen do that on occasion. However, this hardly strikes me as a proper moment to send spirit weapons beyond the Veil.

"Who. Is. Coming?" I growl, clenching my hands into fists.

"Servants of the Master," calls Markesh from my left. He sounds triumphant.

I glance over to see him kneeling on the ground, hands bound behind his back. Two burly men hold on to Markesh's shoulders, pressing down to keep him in place.

"Quiet," orders one of his guards.

"We have sent those you summoned back to the Darklands," I tell Markesh.

His return grin disturbs me. He looks like he knows a secret he's dying to tell us. I wonder if we're about to find out why he volunteered to stay behind and guard us when the others left for the fort.

"Evil comes," warns an old woman gravely.

"Who?" I demand again.

"Denkari," says the woman. Her voice is barely more than a whisper, as if speaking too loudly might bring the evil ones closer.

The Denkari possess bodies much like humans, but they are not human.

"They come for you! All of you! You cannot stop them!" Markesh's laugh shifts into a maniacal giggle, but when he speaks again his voice changes to a smooth, deep, scary voice that does not belong to him. "I am a prophet. Hear my words. The Master comes to find the faithful. Do not fear his loyal servants. Welcome them. Join them. Take up your weapons and capture the magic ones. The faithful shall reap reward. The unfaithful will reap pain and—"

A heavy thunk cuts Markesh off as a small, flat rock flies up and raps him sharply on the forehead. He slumps over unconscious, flopping to the ground as he slips through the startled fingers of his two guards. Unsure of what to do, they simply leave him there.

"That's better." Shadow clears his throat. "How many Denkari are coming? How do you know they will come?"

"I have felt them," declares the same old woman who had spoken before. "They number three for now, and they move closer every moment. Minutes or hours, I could not tell you, but soon."

"What are you going to do about them?" snaps a man. "We cannot fight these devils."

"We know what we have to do," declares a young man. "The prophet said they want the magic ones. There's no reason for any of us to suffer. The other man left when he got that girl, the other traveler. Certainly, the Denkari—"

"He is no prophet," interrupts the old woman. "He is trouble."

I have no desire to hurt these people, but I also have no time to play savior right now. The danger facing Vic grows by the second, and the sense that this new threat stalks her nearly overpowers me.

"Do you want us to fight or are you planning on trading us for your peace?"

"Trade," mumbles half the crowd.

"Fight," cries the other half.

"They are here," says the old woman.

Screams from the back of the crowd confirm her statement.

Our reaction is instantaneous. Shadow's weapons return to him, and he throws up a shield to protect against magic strikes.

Tellen slips through the shield, grabs the three nearest children, and pushes them into the Gathering Hall behind us. Every mother near us hustles her children into the Gathering hall.

Relying on my beetle form, I fly high enough to see three distinct sections of the crowd collapsing, falling forward like wheat felled by a scythe.

Shadow drops the original shield and forms a new one across the threshold to the Gathering Hall. Normal Bereft can still pass through the shield, but unless Shadow drops it, everything with a touch of magic in it, including us, will be kept out.

"Help Tellen," Shadow orders.

Using the nimble dog form, I do as bid, lacking time to raise questions. The crowd milling about in the square bumps into each other. Twice, I dash into the crowd, find a group of three or four villagers, and guide them back to the Gathering Hall. Midway through my third trip, something cold brushes past me and saturates me with hopelessness.

Losing my ability to concentrate, I revert to human form and kneel with my forehead pressed to the ground. Only through massive effort am I able to summon enough willpower to raise my head. My three charges lie prone around me. The wave of hopelessness spreads in front of me.

Three large figures march forward steadily. Their measured footfalls cause pain in everyone unfortunate enough to be in their way.

Shadow releases three spirit arrows in quick succession, but the arrows simply bounce away from the targets and land in the crowd. Frustrated, Shadow banishes the arrows before any damage can be done with them on redirect. With whispered words I cannot hear, Shadow conjures a staff and twirls it to test the balance.

The Denkari on the right and left close in on Shadow from opposite sides.

The one in front and slightly to the left of me pauses to watch.

"Make them submit," growls the Denkari leader. He is not exactly a high-ranking member, but he outranks the other two. His slightly curved silver sword rests idly in his left hand.

I silently thank Master Talini for the lessons on mystical creatures.

Before the fight can begin, Tellen eases up beside Shadow and raises his hands—clutching daggers, of course—toward the Denkari approaching from Shadow's left and my right. I know Tellen wants to fire lightning bolts into these Denkari, but he refrains for the sake of the densely packed crowd trembling all around the creatures.

With the three Denkari focused on my companions, my ability to think returns and a crazy idea springs to mind. If I think about it too long, sanity might prevent me from carrying out the plan. Pushing every thought from my mind, I gather my will and strength to break the mental shackles the Denkari have placed upon me.

The Denkari strike hard and fast, swinging their terrible black blades. The metal on their swords appears etched with bright lines weaving an intricate pattern up and down the blades. The Denkari facing Tellen possesses a blade with brilliant blue etchings, confirming the warrior as a low-ranking officer. The Denkari facing Shadow bears the green-lined blade of a foot soldier.

Shadow meets his opponent directly while Tellen dodges each strike from his opponent. The clanging sound of battle fills the area. As Tellen starts adding careful lightning strikes to distract the Denkari, I yank my attention away from the combatants to concentrate on my task. I need a source of fire, Tellen's cooperation, quick reflexes, solid aim, and a generous share of holy help to carry out my plan.

The battle settles into a rhythm with Tellen and Shadow dancing into and out of range of the Denkari weapons. The creatures miss the opportunity to end the fight quickly.

As my companions begin to grow weary, I charge forward, shouting, "Tellen! The berries! Give me the berries and get a torch for Shadow!"

The distraction nearly gets Shadow killed as he hesitates a quarter of a second too long in blocking a heavy strike targeting his head. Thankfully, his reflexes save him.

Along the way, I snatch up a fallen torch, light it with my fingertips, and call, "Trade!"

Tellen catches on and tosses me the pouch of baydonberries as I pitch the lit torch to him. Thinking I must have lost my mind, I empty the bag onto the ground, turn into a snake, and scoop up as many of the berries as possible. I miss about a third of them, but I cannot waste time on regrets.

One of the beautiful loopholes in transformation is that objects in one's mouth are treated as part of the body, making the baydonberries mine to command. In this case, I simply shrink them and load them into my venom pouch.

Shadow sets up two temporary shields to slow the Denkari down a few seconds. If properly anchored, the shields might have kept the Denkari at bay, but as is, it disorients them for a few seconds. The move earns Tellen and Shadow enough time to get up to the Gathering Hall roof. I'm not sure if they climbed or leapt, but they make it. No wonder Arkonai are so hard to track in a fight. They pause with their heads tilted toward each other, and I know Tellen is explaining my plan to Shadow.

Sharp talons pierce me in five different places, nearly causing me to swallow the baydonberries. Shunting the pain aside, I transform into a beetle and fly straight at the Denkari captain's feet. Once there, I change back to snake form and coil around his legs, tripping him.

The other two Denkari whirl to face me.

I fire a stream of berry-laced venom at each Denkari before turning and biting the captain. Uncoiling and retreating a few feet, I strike again, giving him a bigger dose of the venom. Screams erupt from the other two Denkari as Shadow unloads flaming arrows into them.

Realizing what I've done, the captain dives and rakes my skin with his claws. Furious and in pain, I spit the last of my poison right in his face as Shadow's next flaming arrow rushes to meet it. The sudden burst of flames sears me and dazzles my vision, distracting me from the creature's death throes.

Breathing hard, I let my human form return and find myself sitting on the ground near the body of the fallen Denkari. Pain from deep gashes along both arms and across my back nearly drives me unconscious, but as I begin falling, something catches me.

"That was a sight to behold," Shadow says from somewhere behind me.

Tellen's face appears above me.

"You're absolutely crazy," he declares. Leaning close, he adds, "And you're all right ... for a Saroth." His voice rumbles with amusement and worry. "Rest. We'll get someone to treat these wounds."

His lips brush my forehead as I pass out.

Chapter 15:
Sara

Victoria Saveron
Gabon's Stable, Village of Bright Hope

"What do they want with ya?" Sara inquires. Her soft, lilting accent soothes me as much as the odd smelling paste she's been beating with a thin wooden spoon.

As much as I would like to respond, I am uncertain where to begin and need to concentrate to gather enough strength to voice an answer. Between the lack of sleep, the endless walking, the little sustenance, and the wretched ropes, the day has not been kind to me. My wrists and neck burn from where the ropes punished me for every small movement. My thoughts drift back to Coldhaven and the terrifying screams that reached us when we were well upon the road. I imagine the horrors that came upon my friends and wish I could have aided them or at least perished with them.

They live.

I'm not sure if the thought is wishful thinking or a message, but I accept it at face value for now. There's not a great deal I can do to help them anyway, even if I could stand up straight. Simply shifting to a more comfortable position on the straw takes a lot of effort. The only positive thing I can say for the pain is that it distracts me, putting the pungent smell of animals in perspective.

Tired of waiting, Sara stops mixing and starts chatting again.

"Here we are in this fine mess, and I know naught but yer name and only half at that, assuming ye have a surname." She takes hold of my hands and positions them so she can reach the wounds.

Wincing, Sara gives the paste another round of mixing. "This should help but it's going to sting. Feel free to scream as ya like. I doubt it will bother the beasts, and I've been around enough wee ones to handle a good scream now and then. I'd like to give a good scream about now, but I haven't half the excuse as ye do."

"Thank you." My voice sounds wispy.

"Ye won't be thanking me in a moment," Sara notes, "but the pain will fade, the wounds will heal, and the sun will rise on a better day, as me mum likes to say." As she speaks, Sara covers my wrists with the brown paste. Her touch is gentle, and she doesn't hesitate to touch the unnaturally cool, clammy skin on my diseased hand.

For a brief time, I suffer nothing, and then my good wrist feels like it's been ripped raw then bathed in salt, which I suppose is essentially what has transpired. The other wrist hurts too, but the pain is muted, as if the damaged skin doesn't remember how to convey pain. I clench both hands into fists and bite my lower lip to hold in the scream begging release. My effort turns the scream into a muffled whimper accompanied by tears.

"That's grand it is," Sara encourages. "Just a few more spots to treat and the pain'll be nothing but a memory, a bad memory to be sure, but a thing past."

Sara reaches for each of my ankles and applies a generous portion of the salve to the wounds.

Pain blossoms in my ankles, but the level remains far below that which originally engulfed my good wrist. Our captors' efforts to keep the ankle ropes from doing serious harm paid off for the most part. Somehow experiencing pain from several different areas helps me ignore some of it. Tears flow down my face in greater abundance, despite my efforts to curb them.

"Let the tears come, lass," Sara encourages, brushing damp hair away from my face. "Pay the pain little mind. Here now, ease me curiosity and tell me who ya are."

"Victoria Saveron."

Sara picks up my diseased hand and caresses it.

"Well, Victoria, I'm happy to know ya, even if the introduction was bit rough." She offers me a smile and sets my hand down. "Me full name's Sara Amelia Andari, but Sara does just fine. Soon as I finish patching these wounds, I'll fetch the water and bread the stable boy left for us. And I'll apologize ahead for me cold hands." She pauses for me to respond.

I manage to nod.

Sara gently lifts my shirt enough to use the last of her healing paste to trace the irritated spots around my waist.

"Yer body will feel better after ya have a bite to eat." Her smile brightens, lightening her features. "I always feel better when there's food about, and the people of Bright Hope certainly know how to make a fine loaf of bread. Me elder brother moved out here to learn from the finest baker in these parts." Her smile falters and fades.

The pain across my midsection momentarily drives thoughts away. To distract myself, I cautiously ask, "What happened to him?"

"Winter cough," she replies with a shrug. "Gordy always had weak lungs. They killed his dreams of a soldier's life first, and eventually, they took his body as well. So, now it's me and the folks in our cozy home in Coldhaven."

"I'm sorry," I murmur, grateful the pain has subsided enough to let me think again.

"Ye have nothing to be sorry about," Sara assures. To reinforce her words, she picks up my leathery right hand and clasps it between her two perfect hands. "The One gives and takes as He does. Ours is not the path of sadness but of peace and strength found in living through hardship."

"How can you bear to touch that hand?" I ask.

As she considers the question, Sara lifts her right hand off mine and tucks it beneath her left so that my corrupt hand is displayed between us. When at last she speaks, her answer surprises me.

"It is an honest hand."

My expression earns another smile.

"It shows the darkness and rot awaiting us without the One. Everybody has it. We just don't all show it. When the One comes and claims us, it'll heal, but until then, at least ya have a reminder that ye live by power outside mortal flesh."

"How do you have such strong faith?" I feel ridiculous asking the question. Am I allowed to feel doubt? If anyone deserves to be the Chosen Redeemer, surely this lady should qualify.

"Hold that thought," Sara says, giving my right hand a gentle pat. "It deserves more than a quick answer, and I'm famished. We should eat." A troubled expression crosses her face. "It's a long way to the next village, and we may have to start early again."

I grunt at the unpleasant thought.

With one last, reassuring squeeze, Sara releases my hand and gets up to fetch the food. She's back by my side in moments. Gingerly, she helps me shift to a position better for being fed.

"I hate being helpless," I mutter.

Sara's next words contain a deep streak of wisdom.

"It is no more than we always are. I will explain more as ye eat." She breaks off a bite-sized chunk of bread and holds it close to my mouth.

Not really in an eating mood, but lacking the will to fight her, I open my mouth. The soft bread touches my tongue with a sweetness that nearly brings more tears. I chew slowly and accept another mouthful. Noticing Sara has eaten nothing and probably plans on feeding me the whole lot, I wave off the third bite.

"Yours."

Nodding graciously, Sara closes her eyes then eagerly puts the bread in her mouth. From then on, she alternates giving me a morsel then taking one for herself. As much as possible, she also pours water down my throat.

"What's going to happen when that water runs its natural course?" I wonder, trying to fend off the cup hovering near my lips.

"Yer body is probably dehydrated enough to prevent the need, but just in case, there's a bucket over there." She points toward the entrance.

"Lovely."

Sara's rolling laughter lightens something inside me.

"There are worse fates than a bucket in a barn." A renewed sense of our situation settles on her, driving off most of the joy, but an inexplicable serenity still surrounds her. Placing the cup on the ground, she says, "Ye never did tell me what they want with ya, but first, I've an explanation to deliver, if the interest is still there."

"It's still there." Relieved to not have to drink any more, I settle back to listen to Sara explain why she possesses such unshakable faith in the One. I want to tell her about my dream, the prophecy, and everything else. For some reason, her opinion matters much to me.

Finding a comfortable patch of hay, Sara sits down, clasps her hands around her knees, and leans toward me.

"When the One made the world, it was perfect, but after the Outcast's rebellion, his corruption poisoned everything. I have faith because the One called me."

"Out loud?" I wonder, thinking perhaps we have more in common than I know.

Sara shakes her head.

"No. Here and here." She points to her head and heart. My disappointment must show on my face, for Sara chuckles. "I know it's hard to believe, but He chose me, Sara Andari of Coldhaven."

My attention snaps back into place.

"Chose you, how? For what?" I don't mean to be rude, but I need answers. My breath catches as I wait.

Sara looks embarrassed.

"It's a silly notion, but now that I know it's true, I'm flattered and scared and excited."

"What's a silly notion?" I demand. Her reaction makes no sense.

Trying to contain tears of joy, Sara gushes, "Since the time I was small, I always thought I would find the one. Not the One, of course, but His representative here. The signs are set. Nothing else needs to happen. Sometimes, I think I can see and hear The Lady, blessed be her name, telling me my wait will soon be over."

"What signs? How do you know the being you hear is The Lady?"

"The dark ones return in great numbers," Sara answers. "That is one sign. There are other signs, including you. As for The Lady's voice, you will know her when you hear her call."

"How am I a sign?"

Crawling over to me, Sara tucks her knees beneath her and reaches for my wrists. "These," she says, running her hands down my bracers, "are the mark of the Chosen Redeemer." As her fingertips reach the edges of my bracers, Sara's head drops into a bow and her eyes focus on a time and place I cannot see.

I scarcely dare to breathe as I wait for whatever may come.

When Sara finally speaks, her voice is that same low, melodious, ageless voice I've heard before.

"The One's Chosen Redeemer will walk the land when the Corruption reaches its peak. The Chosen Redeemer will suffer greatly, defy death, and use Kailon's Gift to banish the Outcast's army, redeem the lost, and heal the broken."

I have no problem with the end of the prophecy, but the beginning is very scary.

Chapter 16:
The Long Road to Fort Amareth

The Lady
Coldhaven to Bright Hope to Coolwater Creek to Fort Amareth
In wolf form, Adam Castillo tracks Oren's party from one village to the next. As often as possible, I let my spirit linger with him, renewing his strength and resolve in the mission. Leaving his twin sister to face the Denkari with two Arkonai companions has wounded something inside him. Though Katrina has no knowledge of him, Adam has always been aware of her. Visions of what he might say to Katrina once he reveals himself fill Adam's head as he races through the forest. He does not doubt that she will somehow free herself, but he despises having to quit a battle before it begins.

Adam and his sister grew up within a day's ride of each other, but their circumstances could hardly have been more different. Fearing what the political enemies Marcus gathered by the dozen would do to her son, their mother—Gabriella—sent Adam away with a dear friend when the boy was only a month old.

One would think keeping such a secret an impossibility, but a combination of Saroth isolation customs and my favor let the plan succeed. So Adam grew up as the son of Maggie and Aldo Castillo, humble tenant farmers on the Polani lands, and his twin sister, Katrina, grew up in her father's house. Sadly, their mother's fears proved well-founded and assassins struck Gabriella down before Katrina had reached her third birthday.

Although both Maggie and Aldo possessed minimal power, they knew Adam's bloodline would guarantee tremendous power. They told the boy of his heritage on his seventh birthday, just before sending him to the Alamon Temple to be tested by the monks.

Under my influence, Adam found his way to Master Patros who taught him the Shapeshifter arts. Even as he poured himself into his training, Adam also devoted much time to researching his blood kin. The fact that Marcus Polani's influence stretched far and wide made the research a simple matter.

Katrina almost ended up at the Alamon Temple to study under Master Patros, but I feared the strong bond between the twins would reveal the truth far too soon and endanger them both. So I sent Master Talini to offer her services, so Katrina could train from home. Master Patros would have been good for Katrina, but I find no fault in the training Master Talini provided the girl. Katrina's speed at switching among her three forms can barely be matched by masters with twenty-plus years of experience.

Though only able to master wolf form, Adam's tradecraft borders on perfection. When placed among a real pack of wolves and three other students in wolf form for comparison, only Master Patros recognized him after nearly a half-hour of steady observation. The other three students were identified within the first ten minutes by every master. Adam blended well enough to fool four of the five masters present. It was a proud moment for the young man.

Tapping into this pleasant memory, I channel the sense of pride and accomplishment to spur Adam on. I can only offer him determination and hope during this lonely task.

Unfortunately, I cannot provide details about what will come. I know only that the Denkari are not the worst Jackson Castaloni can—and will—summon if given half a chance. His plans for Vic most likely involve taking her to the dungeons below Fort Amareth where a dormant Darkland portal is rumored to be. How he will treat the Arkonai remains obscured in the nebulous nature of the future. Jordan Lekros will do his utmost to stop Jackson for his own reasons, but I hesitate to count him a committed ally.

When Oren's party stops in Bright Hope, Adam hunts a pair of rabbits for his supper. Since he cannot risk a fire this close to the village, he stays in wolf form as he consumes them. In his wolf form he possesses the Sight, and thus, he can see the spiritual and emotional states of each person. However, his touch upon those spirits can only convey basic messages. Adam briefly debates himself over whether or not he should take on his human form or remain a wolf. He finally decides he should remain as a wolf, for that is the state where he can gain the most information quickly.

Throughout the night, I send Adam around to each of the faithful within Bright Hope so he can prepare them. Tucked up warm in their beds, most do not stir at his first call, but a few feel his presence and respond by lighting the vigilance lamps.

Once Adam rouses enough people, they spread the word on their own, freeing him to hold a vigil near the stable where Sara and Vic sleep. At this point, he hesitates, for he longs to free them.

I prevent him from doing so for several reasons. Should Oren find them missing, the innocents of Bright Hope will suffer. Also, with the threat of Jackson Castaloni's arrival pending, the village cannot afford to be divided. Finally, Vic and Sara need to rest as long as possible.

As the level of activity rises around the village, Adam's fear that Oren may rise and flee with his captives becomes more justified. A low, plaintive whine escapes Adam as he watches the flickering, gray spirit forms of Sara and Vic. The dull cast to their forms indicates that both girls are still dangerously exhausted. He silently pleads for my intervention.

I consider the request and grant it. Working through Adam, I channel strength to bolster their spirits, trying to heal them just enough to see them through. I would love to open myself fully to them, but the moment is not right. They would not know what to do with such power, nor would the village people be ready to receive them in their true forms.

As I finish, Adam's heightened senses detect approaching footsteps. He presses his body deeper into the shadows next to the stable holding Sara and Vic. A growl builds in his throat as he smells Oren, Ederon, and Lerik approaching. Adam crouches and his muscles coil. Hot blood pounds through him. Every part of him wants to bring a swift end to Oren. His mind automatically plans how he can best conquer these three opponents.

Although the sentence of death would be justified in Oren's case, doing so now would only bring the sort of divisiveness that could doom Bright Hope's chances of surviving the next few hours.

My belief in Adam's ability to control his instinct to kill does not waver, but I gently remind him of his duty anyway. His mind balks at letting Oren walk away with the girls, but he obeys and remains still while Vic and Sara are bound and forced to march down the main road.

When it becomes safe to do so, Adam moves to a new position so he can watch the strange parade.

Despite the late hour the street slowly fills with silent witnesses, both young and old. Most appear confused, some frightened, and still others frown deeply, but nobody dares to oppose Oren, who rides ahead of the procession of three horses.

The prisoners plod on behind. Adam cannot see their expressions, but the slightly brighter cast to their auras encourages him.

Midway down the street, Ederon leans over and hauls Sara onto his horse. I expect the same to happen to Victoria as the party's pace is dictated by how quickly she can walk, and Oren's impatience is obvious. Upon drawing even with the last house on the main road out of the village, Lerik hauls Victoria up onto his horse, and the party gallops away.

When they are out of sight, Adam relaxes. I send him into the stable for a long drink and a mouse to snack on. Thus strengthened, Adam presses on.

The horses force Oren's group to stay on the main road, but Adam shares no such restrictions. Free to find the best path, Adam dashes ahead of the party so he can warn the people of Coolwater Creek before Oren arrives.

Just before dawn, the group reaches Coolwater Creek where Oren lets his men and prisoners rest and eat while he handles some business with the villagers. He manages to barter for five fresh mounts, but otherwise, the people seem annoyed with him, rather than fearful. Oren has no way of knowing Adam arrived before him and prepared the people for trouble.

The exit from Coolwater Creek bears eerie similarities to the march through Bright Hope. Starting at one end of the longest street, Vic and Sara are slowly paraded through the village while families watch in horrified little huddles. This time, however, when Ederon tries to get Sara onto the mount obtained for her, Sara refuses and continues walking beside Victoria. Though the gesture is a small thing, pride sweeps through me.

Tucked in the crowd in human form, Adam indulges in a smile as he watches Sara and Victoria lifted up onto separate horses. Then, as the villagers begin milling about questioning each other on what has transpired, Adam slips away to a private spot to become a wolf again.

For the last leg of the journey, Adam follows behind the horses in Oren's band, stopping when they stop and pressing on when they do. Once he settles into a steady pace, he lets his thoughts wander back to his sister and the two Arkonai huntsmen with her, fervently hoping they stop Jackson Castaloni.

At one point, Adam stops on the crest of a hill and looks back at Bright Hope and Coolwater Creek, tiny and idyllic in appearance from this distance. Though his wolf eyes are sharper than his human ones, Adam assumes his human form to peer down at the two villages, one far to his left and one to his right.

"Will I see them like this again?" Curiosity and sadness tinge his voice as he addresses me.

"Many changes will come, but there is hope that when you see them again, they will be better than they are in this moment," I answer, speaking directly into his mind.

Returning to wolf form, Adam again takes up the chase. He does not return to his human form until he stands on the edge of Bleakwood Forest, eyes fixed upon the impressive, vine-covered walls of Fort Amareth.

Sara Andari - Coldhaven Villager

Chapter 17:
Family Reunion

Victoria Saveron
Courtyard Ruins, Fort Amareth

A heavy feeling comes upon me as soon as the horse carrying me crosses the threshold into Fort Amareth's courtyard.

A glance at Sara tells me she feels worse than I do. The pale girl looks ready to attend an undead formal event, and despite her firm grip on the saddle pommel, I suspect a slight breeze could knock her head-first off the mount.

This place feels wrong. Even though it's only mid-afternoon, the life seems drained from this place. The courtyard appears abandoned, but the high stone walls have many places to hide people. Thick moss softens large swatches of stone edges, yet there's nothing soft about this place. Somehow, the shadows seem deeper than normal, like they hold dark, ancient secrets. I imagine eyes watching us from every side.

Nervously, I eye the evil-looking patches of dirt scattered about the courtyard that appear ready to disgorge hordes of undead. I wonder what will happen if we're attacked now. The ropes binding me to the saddle hold me well enough under normal circumstances, but I doubt my special bracers would fail me just because of a short length of rope.

Although I try not to think about dying, I find the notion of perishing while tied up and presented like a war trophy frustrating.

"My contract has been fulfilled."

I flinch as Oren's voice shatters the stillness. A shot of fear drives off most of the sick feeling that had my guts in knots.

"So I see, well done, Huntmaster Oren," praises Supreme Huntmaster Jordan Lekros. He emerges from the deep shadows to my right. "I'm surprised my son is not with you. Is there a reason for that?" The Arkonai leader's controlled tone conveys a challenge. His stance remains casual, but there's a stillness about him that tells us he's more than ready to strike.

Sara gasps. I can only stare dumbly at Lekros, and hope my mouth doesn't drop open like a fish given a good squeeze. Throughout the journey Sara and I vainly tried to get Oren to explain the details of his contract. Finding Oren's leash held by the Supreme Huntmaster—leader of the Arkonai Hunting Guild and the closest thing my father's people have to royalty—is beyond unnerving. It doesn't make sense. I might be an embarrassment to some Arkonai because of my mother, but that hardly warrants a contract.

"My contract was for the girl, not your son," Oren says evenly. "Give me my due, and I'll take my leave."

"Yes, your contract was for Daniel's girl, but I find myself presented with two young ladies. Do you care to explain?" The glare leveled at Oren contradicts the casual tone of the Supreme Huntmaster's words. He may not know Sara specifically, but he knows what her role has been.

Two seconds pass as Oren returns the Supreme Huntmaster's gaze, but finally, he explains.

"The contract had a few … complications. The second girl is a hostage to keep the first one in line. Besides, it keeps the people of Coldhaven in check as well." His explanation comes out with slow, sarcastic patience.

I frown at Oren, annoyed that he's speaking about Sara and me like we're stray pups he's explaining to his daddy.

With a deep sigh Supreme Huntmaster Lekros rubs his head wearily.

"This must stop, Oren. You cannot continue endangering Bereft."

"He's done this before?" I ask, surprising everybody. "What else have you done?" I demand of Oren, remembering Tellen's comment about him being known as *Destroyer*.

Both men ignore me. My cheeks flush from frustration and the sun's harsh attention. Despite the many shadows cast by the high walls, the sun rules over the courtyard's center. Sweat builds up under the ropes, settling on the raw areas and generally making me miserable.

Then, a cool breeze from the surrounding plains climbs the wall and blows through the courtyard, offering me relief.

"I finish my contracts," Oren points out defensively.

"Your actions are starting to cost us contracts," Lekros retorts. "Take your followers and return the girl to wherever you got her. I don't mind who you hire to fulfill your contracts, but from now on, no more innocents."

The laughter that bubbles out of Oren contains mockery and mirth.

"You're in no position to speak about innocents," Oren notes, gesturing at me. "You should be thanking me for taking the contract on Daniel's whelp. You know nobody else would. I hear even your own son dragged his feet on taking the contract. Now, pay me."

Reaching into his pocket, Supreme Huntmaster Lekros withdraws a small pouch tied with a thin piece of twine. With a casual flip, he tosses the pouch at Oren's feet. The impact loosens the twine enough to let several silver coins spill out. The clinking noise strikes an odd chord in me. These coins—a surprising number of them—have been spent for my capture. Again the questions: *Who would bother?* and *Why me?* fill my head.

When Oren bends down to pick up his payment, Lekros moves almost faster than I can follow. One moment he's standing stock-still a couple of meters away and the next instant he's standing over Oren with his dagger pressed under the man's chin.

"We have rules for a reason. Either abide by them or accept the consequences. You may be good, but you cannot always be perfect. Blacklisting will be the least of your problems if you defy me again. Do you understand?"

"I understand," Oren answers, swallowing carefully.

"What does he understand?" The speaker's measured tone adds: *I have a few more questions and you'd better have really good answers for them.*

The sound of my father's question coming from behind me fills me with joy and fear. I try to turn to look at him, but the disagreeable horse sidesteps, making me concentrate on not falling off. By the time I recover my balance and still the horse, my father stands between me and the men exchanging money for my life.

For a short time, everything is right in the world. Then, several things happen. Lerik and Ederon—who I clearly forgot about—move their horses up beside Sara and me, slash the ropes holding us to the saddles, knock us off, leap down, and press daggers to our necks.

Well, this is a fine mess.

Strangely, I want to laugh, and I'm definitely entertaining some dagger envy. It doesn't matter that I'd probably be more of a danger to myself than anybody else with a dagger. Everybody else seems to have one. Maybe I'm finally losing the last shreds of sanity I have left after this week.

"We were just concluding Oren's contract," Lekros explains, pulling his dagger back and tucking it away.

"The contract *you* put on *my* daughter," my father adds. "Why would you do that?"

Oren gathers the rest of his money, shoves it back in the bag, and climbs to his feet. Nodding to the Supreme Huntmaster, Oren backs away and offers him a mock bow. "A pleasure doing business with—"

"If you move from that spot without permission, I will kill you," interrupts Lekros. His eyes pin Oren in place and his right hand hovers near one of the throwing daggers on his belt. Without shifting his gaze, he addresses my father. "Oren's contract was only so I could fulfill my contract, for you. So the deal is simply this, you surrender, and Victoria is free to go."

"Done," declares my father.

"No!" I cry at the same time. Lerik presses down on my left shoulder to keep me in place and moves his blade so that a thin cut opens on my neck, but I don't care.

"Good!" cheers Lekros. "Oren, kill him. Then you may go."

"Hypocrite," mutters Oren, drawing his dagger.

"It's bad form to kill a man without at least telling him why he must die," scolds a jolly, silky voice from behind us, "especially if he's kin."

"Jack!" exclaims my father. Though his voice holds surprise, a faint note of hope also exists. The hope vanishes beneath suspicion when my father asks, "What's going on?"

A man dressed in black walks into my line of sight and faces my father, careful to stay out of reach. This must be Uncle Jack, my mother's younger brother, the Conjurer. He's thin and pale and sickly looking. I've never met him, but I've certainly heard of him.

"You'll die soon, Daniel, but not this exact moment," informs Uncle Jack. "You deserve it for corrupting my sister, but I need a moment to enjoy the triumph." His dark eyes, which seem to suck in light, widen in horror. "Be a good man and let Oren bind you so I don't have to kill you prematurely."

Oren glances at Lekros who confirms the order with a nod. Looking mystified, Oren fetches some rope from one of the horses, forces my father to sit down, and binds his hands and feet.

"That's better," comments Uncle Jack.

"Get on with it," grouses the Supreme Huntmaster.

Clearly enjoying himself, Uncle Jack asks my father, "Did you know that your illustrious Supreme Huntmaster has the same grandfather as you? Do you know why this fact is important?"

"Let Victoria and the other girl go, Jack." My father sounds weary.

I want to hold him and let him protect me.

Uncle Jack's expression flips from playful to dangerous.

"Don't spoil the fun, Daniel, or I'll have to hurt one of them."

A yelp from Sara tells me Ederon's done something to emphasize Uncle Jack's point.

Seething, my father shoves his next several breaths through clenched teeth. Then, forcing himself to be calm, he says, "No, I did not know that. Why should it matter?"

"The bracers," whispers Lekros.

"The bracers," Uncle Jack echoes. His eyes gleam as he stares at my bracers. "We both seek them, but—"

"Take them!" I shout. Blood pounds so hard in my temple, I think something might burst soon. A scream gets locked in my throat, burning like I'd swallowed a boiling potato.

"No, Victoria," Sara whispers. "They're the only things preventing the turning."

"I don't care!" I snap. "Take the bracers!" I scream at Uncle Jack and the Supreme Huntmaster, holding my arms as far out as the ropes will allow. "Let him go! Stop threatening people!" I stop speaking because anything else will simply be raving.

"Brave, but pointless," says Uncle Jack. "There is the matter of succession."

"What does—"

I don't get to finish my question because Sara's sharp intake of breath tells me she already has the answer.

"Well, go on, girl, don't keep them waiting for enlightenment," Uncle Jack prompts.

"Vic doesn't own the bracers," my father says flatly. He shifts so he can look at me. "I do." Tearing his eyes from me, he looks to Uncle Jack and Lekros. "Kill me for whatever reason you think right, but let her keep the bracers for three more years. When she's a woman in full, she may be able to live without them."

Uncle Jack draws in a breath, holds it a moment, and releases it.

"Ah, the sweet sounds of pleading. Magnificent." Beaming, he waves toward my father. "Supreme Huntmaster, I believe the contract can now be fulfilled, but do the honors yourself."

Pursing his lips in annoyance, Lekros pulls out two of his throwing daggers and flicks them at my father.

Sara and I both scream.

Chapter 18:
Awakening

Victoria Saveron
Courtyard Ruins to Lower Dungeons, Fort Amareth

I lunge towards my father, straining at the length of rope connecting my wrists and neck.

Lerik's quick reflexes save me from splitting my neck open upon his blade or strangling myself. Instead of killing me, his dagger bites most of the way through the rope around my neck. The last strands constrict about my throat, causing my vision to blacken as my body fights off unconsciousness. With desperate strength, I yank downward with both wrists, snapping the few remaining strands. Sweet, tepid air floods my lungs and my eyes immediately seek my father.

Spots dance around my blurry vision, making the scene before me difficult to understand. This is nothing like waking after a battle, at least then my senses are clear.

A large wolf lies draped across my father's fallen form. I cannot see either of their faces, but they're not moving. For a moment, I can only sit on the ground, pull air into my aching lungs, and listen to my heart pound in my ears.

"Free their ankles. We need to move them to the portal," says Uncle Jack, sounding like he's speaking through water. He frowns deeply, but I can't spare the emotion to be satisfied by it.

Scrambling forward, using my elbows to drag my bound feet along the ground, I cover half the distance to my father before something heavy—Lerik—lands on top of my back. What little breath

I have left gushes from my body, leaving me no strength to resist as Lerik hauls me to my knees, cuts the ropes around my ankles, and yanks me to my feet. I'm afraid to look at my father's still form, but I must.

From a standing position, I see one of the throwing daggers lodged in my father's left shoulder and the other buried at the base of the wolf's thick neck. Blood flows from both wounds, staining the wolf's shiny fur, my father's shirt, and the stones and dust beneath them. Grunting with effort, my father struggles to shift the wolf's body off his chest.

"Help him!" I snap at everybody watching my father's efforts to free himself, momentarily forgetting they had just tried to kill him. "Get it off him." My voice drops to a horrified whisper.

Where did the wolf come from?

Suddenly, I remember seeing this wolf in the Karnok Mountains.

The wolf whimpers.

Uncle Jack figures it out first.

"Take the dagger out and we'll find out. He's a Shapeshifter."

Ederon leaves his post guarding Sara to do as Uncle Jack suggests. Approaching from behind, Ederon grips the small dagger's handle with one hand and braces himself against the wolf's side with the other.

As soon as the blade slides free, the wolf morphs into a young man with jet black hair and a deep gash on top of his left shoulder very close to the base of his neck.

Supreme Huntmaster Lekros motions and Ederon pulls the wounded man upright. Despite the pain it must cause him, the young man twists away and casts pale blue eyes upon me. As our eyes meet, I feel like I should know him, though I'm sure we've never met. Annoyed, Ederon grips the young man's arm, marches him over to Lekros, and forces him to kneel before the Arkonai leader.

Knowing Lerik must be distracted, I kick back and connect with his left shin. Unfortunately, we're too close for me to do any real damage, but he loosens his grip enough for me to break free and go to my father. I'm by his side just long enough to pull the dagger out and toss it away. If I had been thinking clearer, I would have kept the dagger, but the urge to get it as far away as possible proves too strong. Then, Lerik's at my side, again pulling me up as my father continues to bleed at my feet.

"You should have left the dagger in," Lerik comments. He sounds almost sorry. "There's nothing you can do now. Arkonai throwing daggers are almost always poisoned."

A strong denial gets lost in the panic growing in my mind. My breaths come quicker now but somehow each yields less useful air than the last.

"Question the boy later. We should move now," Uncle Jack insists.

Lerik's grip loosens slightly as he pushes me toward the yawning entrance to the fort's main structure.

"No!" I shout, twisting my body violently to wrench my arm free. "Let me stay with him!" Tears nearly blind me.

"Control her!" Lekros yells with disgust.

"How? She's not even thinking right now," grumbles Lerik.

The left side of my head explodes with pain as a fist slams into my temple above my eye. Everything blanks out, yet I'm strangely aware of falling. Opening my eyes causes more pain and dizziness, so I shut my eyes and try to remember how to stand. Hands catch me under my arms and begin dragging me.

I'm not sure how the rest of the journey to the lower dungeons proceeds. By the time the world stops spinning, I'm kneeling in the center of a large, sand-covered pit, staring listlessly up at Uncle Jack.

"Wake up, Victoria," Uncle Jack orders, gently patting my cheek. "Now's not the time for rest. Give me the bracers."

Though still confused, I have enough strength and sense to shake my head.

"I'm trying to spare you for Alec's sake, but I could take the bracers off your cold, dead corpse," says Uncle Jack impatiently.

Who's Alec? I wonder.

"I can't." My voice sounds as empty as I feel inside.

"You can and you will, or I'll have—"

The new threat sends hot anger coursing to every part of my body, clearing the fog from my mind.

"I can't!" I repeat, sharpening my gaze on Uncle Jack. "They've hardly been off a day since I got them. Most times they don't even let me take them off." Holding my hands out to him, I add, "Go on. Try to take them off."

The bracers are currently in their thin form, appearing to be nothing more than ornate metal bracelets, fancy cuffs holding me prisoner. However, as soon as Uncle Jack touches them, the bracers take on their defensive form, covering my forearms. A sudden tingling in my teeth warns me of something dark approaching a half-second before the bracers light up.

"What's happening?" Lekros barks the question at Uncle Jack in a tone that adds: *What else can go wrong with this plan?*

"It's starting! They're ready. Open the portal, my dear." Uncle Jack looks positively gleeful.

"I don't—" I cut myself off as the knowledge floods me.

Do as he says. I will be with you. The thoughts come complete with that same strange, ageless female voice. In one flash of inspiration, The Lady explains what mere mortals cannot understand. Uncle Jack wants me to open the Darkland portals, but I am the Chosen Redeemer, I can access more than that evil place. I can reach the Veil to Kailon's homeland.

"You may not know, but those bracers know their purpose," Uncle Jack whispers reverently, breaking into my thoughts. "Open the portal or watch as I have Ederon gut the girl and Lerik tear the boy's heart out to throw at your feet."

"That is disgusting," I mutter. Oddly, the threat helps me think. "Why would the Arkonai help you anyway?" He doesn't answer the question. "Untie me."

Uncle Jack stares like he's trying to see within me to root out deception.

"You still have your hostages," I remind my uncle.

"That's—"

"I can't fulfill your order until the bracers are uninhibited," I say, cutting off Lekros's objection. Honestly, I have no idea where the fancy words or calm tone come from, but they seem right.

After another long stare, Uncle Jack conjures a small knife and cuts the ropes holding my hands together. Through great effort, I remain perfectly still to spare the two prisoners painful deaths.

"May I stand?" My leg muscles burn from kneeling so long.

Uncle Jack waves permission and steps aside so he's not standing in front of me anymore.

Closing my eyes, I stretch forth my hands and speak the ancient words filling my mind. "Hama, portoolen esto negmon. Hama, shato efin pece. Celastra enselema, adictudo: alam." In the common language, the words mean, "Hear me, gateway to lands best forgotten. Hear me, path to a better place. With the power entrusted to me, I command thee both: open."

At first my arms stiffen, but then they move of their own accord. My right forearm crosses over my left forearm. The sound of howling wind engulfs me. Fingers splayed wide, light gushes from the bracers through my hands and begins forming two glowing, blue-white rings side by side in the air above my crossed arms.

I feel like I'm swimming, and my arms waver as my body trembles to contain the energy using me as a conduit. The portals start from the bottom, where the bracers' light focuses, then split and arc upward, carving a curved path that swings out symmetrically to both sides and meets at the top.

Once formed, the two portals descend until they are inches above the ground and move like doors on hinges, angling away from each other. The energy flowing from the bracers slows and stops. As I get to the open command, the portals appear transparent, letting us gaze into foreign lands.

The portal on my left shows a dark place filled with fire and lined with masses of undead waiting to cross over. The sight can do nothing but drain one of hope. The portal on my right offers a glimpse into a green place full of life and lined with white-robed warriors armed with gleaming swords.

A second slowly stretches as the captains of both armies eye each other grimly. Then, together, they step through to begin their battle.

Uncle Jack lets out a bloodcurdling scream.

"What have you done?" He spins me around to look at me.

I smile.

"Kill them!" Uncle Jack cries.

Parts of my spirit I never knew awaken, and my smile widens as I spring into action.

Chapter 19:
Chosen Redeemer

Victoria Saveron
Lower Dungeons, Fort Amareth

This is the first fight I remember. A thought carries me to Sara's side in an instant, just as Ederon hears the kill order. As his hand twitches to obey, I catch it with my right hand and squeeze. A bright flash fills the room around us. Sara's surprised cry immediately gets overridden by Ederon's panicked, pain-filled scream as pure white light flows through my bracer down my hand into his wrist. I let go and Ederon recoils, stumbling backward and slamming his head against the stone wall.

After confirming Sara is safe, I seek the wounded young man who intercepted a dagger for my father. I do not know whether my father yet lives, but I cannot spare the time to consider the possibility of his death. Two fates lie before me. I could check on my father and let the battle play out as it will, or I can do what he would do.

Spotting the young man, I leap across the distance between us and place my hands over the deep gash running along his left shoulder. Another white flash surrounds us as the wound closes. He cries out as the power flowing through him burns away the poison. As soon as the healing completes, he transforms into a wolf, bows to me, and rushes to join the fray.

As I consider where to best apply myself, the fight comes to me. Three undead armed with spirit swords rush at me. I duck the first zombie's sword and catch the second's side swing on my left bracer. The evil weapon explodes, flinging shards everywhere. I open my mouth to scream, but no sound emerges, only more white light which

100

destroys every speck that was the spirit sword.

My three foes cower and cover their eyes. The wolf crashes into the lot of them and they disappear in a cloud of dark dust. Before I can thank the wolf, he dashes off to challenge a Denkari advancing on Sara.

Another Denkari leaps at me from behind. Sensing the danger, I move instinctively, dropping into a crouch and ducking so that the creature's attack carries it well over my body. Using my left hand for balance, I glance up and prepare for a renewed attack.

It's almost too late. The Denkari's twin spirit swords are already swinging toward me. I shake my right hand like one would to throw off water and a blade about the length of my bracer drops out, protruding a hand's length beyond my fingertips. Marveling at the new weapon, I jump forward and swing up, driving the blade deep under the Denkari's chin.

The creature's dying scream jangles every nerve, but that's nothing compared to the burning sensation coming from everywhere his black blood touches. A thought sends a strong pulse up and down my bracers, cleansing me of the corrupt lifeblood. Nevertheless, I proceed into the next few fights with more caution.

"Close the dark portal!" shouts the commander of the white-robed soldiers.

I don't need a special address to know he's talking to me, but the order's not exactly easy to carry out. First, I have no idea how to close the portal. Second, there must be sixty beings between me and my goal. Third, I'm suddenly tired to the point where I don't think I can take three more steps let alone fight my way to the Darkland portal. Fourth, what's the point?

As I feel myself falling, Sara catches me, eases me to the ground, and whispers in my ear.

"Guard your mind with The Lady's grace. Keep the faith. Fight on. My prayers are with ye. Now go." The Coldhaven girl plucks me off the ground and pushes me forward.

Her words have a renewing effect on me, and the doubts melt from my mind. I still do not know how I will accomplish my task, but somehow the worry matters less now.

As expected, the first step is the hardest, but the second soon follows and a third. I dodge the first fighting pair and sidestep another. A zombie confronts me soon thereafter, but before I can raise my arms to defend or attack, it drops dead with a throwing dagger in its neck.

Backtracking the blade, I meet Tellen's gaze. He grins but waves impatiently to let me know I should continue.

As I jog forward a few more steps, zombies fall at my feet, felled by a shadowy blur moving swiftly in front of me. I quicken my pace, ducking and dodging as necessary, until I'm directly in front of the Darkland portal. Here, I hesitate as three more zombies emerge from the dark, swirling mist making up the portal. Fear paralyzes me. I sink to my knees halfway between both portals.

My ears feel blocked, and my thoughts mock me with questions and doubts. What if I can't close the portal? Who am I to stand before such glorious power? I am nobody special. Should I die today, tomorrow will simply dawn without me. Then, I hear absolutely nothing, as the sounds of the battle raging around me cease to matter. My eyes are drawn to the bright portal's light.

The silence stretches on for I know not how long, but then, out of that silence comes a strong yet gentle masculine voice.

"Fear not, dear daughter. I have chosen you for such a time as this. Stretch forth your hands and let my power right this wrong."

I'm not advocating for always listening to the voices in your head, but when the One speaks, listen.

Once I stretch forth my hands, palm out, an invisible force wrenches me toward the Darkland portal. For the briefest moment, fear seizes my heart, and I think I'm going to die. I grip both sides of the misty portal's edges and scream as my back feels like a sword has been thrust through it.

"Hang on, Vic!" Tellen's shout sounds far away even though I can feel his presence right beside me.

The pain changes several times, first feeling hot, then cold, then like a stream of warm water flowing through me. My hands clench around the sides of the Darkland portal and pull inward. A zombie ducks under my left arm then tries to remove that arm with his sword, but Tellen defends me again.

An alarmed shout rings through my mind, giving me a headache.

A figure suddenly fills my vision. He's the most beautiful being I've ever seen. His long, golden hair gleams in stark contrast to his dark clothes. His face is filled with love, compassion, and sadness.

"Why do you fight me, Victoria?" he asks in a voice I could listen to all day. "Join me. I can give you this world and the next dozen beside."

Visions of several worlds appear before me. Some are cold and lifeless, while others teem with life.

"I can make every desire come true," the man continues. "I can save everyone you love. No more pain. No more strife. Just let go."

My father's face floats before me. Soon after, my friends appear beside him. They smile and nod like I should trust the man.

Something nags at me.

Liar.

I am fairly certain I don't say the word aloud, as I'm not even sure it's from me, but the man responds anyway.

He places a hand over his heart and closes his eyes as if blinking back pain.

"You wound me, Victoria." Cocking his head left, he adds, "We could be such friends, you and I. Rulers. Conquerors. Saviors. You could access power greater than you can imagine."

I shake my head, though part of me wants to believe him.

With a deep sigh, he says, "I try to be good. I try to be kind. I really do, but sometimes, people don't listen. That hurts. That hurts me a lot, Victoria." The man reaches out as if to caress my right cheek, but as his icy fingers make contact, countless images vie for my attention.

Everyone I love lies dead in a disturbingly perfect line. Everything I hold dear shatters as I watch. The faces of strangers appear then disappear in a haze of fire. Death and destruction fill me until I want to curl up and die to make the images stop.

"What will it be?" inquires the beautiful man.

I come to my senses and find myself on my knees before the Darkland portal, both arms still outstretched and clinging to the edges.

"Speak," commands the man, glaring at me.

Drawing a deep breath, I think of my friends and everything that brought us to this moment.

"You should have stuck with the lies." With that, I draw on the strength offered by the bright portal and pour light into the Darkland portal. With all my strength, I pull the edges of the portal together until the two sides meet. As the sides touch, the portal collapses on itself, drawing every eye to the center of the wide arena. Then, just as suddenly, a shockwave of dark energy bursts outward, flattening everything in its path, including me.

I tumble backwards and roll several times. When I finally stop rolling, it's all I can do to simply suck air into my uncooperative lungs.

Chapter 20:
War Ahead

Katrina Polani
Lower Dungeons, Fort Amareth

It is over, for now. Vic's triumph sucks the will from the few enemies left on the battlefield. Tellen blows apart two of the last three zombies, and Shadow sends an arrow through the last.

Silence rules as the white-clad warriors gather their wounded and retreat to their portal. They wear the faces of mortal men but there's something distinctly different about them. It's like they're a race of perfected humans. They walk with the confidence of righteous purpose. When the last warrior steps through, the portal closes with a gentle rush of wind. I am grateful for this as my bones still ache from the destruction of the dark portal. I cannot complain though, for I escaped the worst of it by having been in snake form at the time of collapse.

My thoughts dwell on the land in the light portal. What little I saw of that peaceful place ignites a longing in me. As I recall how the last bits of light faded, I feel I should know the place.

I use dog form to cross to where Vic has fallen. Tellen arrives on Vic's other side as I reach her. Shadow already kneels beside her head. The wolf stands guard over Vic's uncle a few meters away, growling every time he moves.

Oren and Lerik are nowhere to be found, which I suspect is because they left before the battle got underway. Ederon leans back against the far wall where he fell early in the fight. He is barely conscious. Sara stands above him, telling him to keep still so she can check his head wound. Supreme Huntmaster Lekros limps up the stone stairs, headed for the courtyard. I want to chase him, but I cannot leave Vic like this. Having been closest to the blast, it is no wonder she is last to recover.

"Should we go after him?" Tellen asks, looking at me.

"Don't bother," Shadow says tersely. "I can find him later."

I nod, remembering Shadow's lineage.

"Father," Vic whispers.

At first, I think she speaks of Supreme Huntmaster Lekros being Shadow's father, but then, the real meaning strikes me like an errant bolt of Tellen's lightning. Vic probably does not even know about the connection between Lekros and Shadow.

Taking on dog form, I dash across the arena, up the stone stairs, and through the long hallways until I burst into the courtyard. To my relief, I find the wolf standing sentinel over Vic's father.

The Supreme Huntmaster stands a few meters away, dagger in hand as he contemplates the odds of fighting the wolf. For his part, the beautiful wolf growls low in his throat at every cautious step the Arkonai leader takes.

I bark fiercely to announce my arrival, though the Supreme Huntmaster is already adjusting his position to account for me. My presence causes him to reconsider the odds. Slipping his dagger away, he runs over to one of the horses wandering around the courtyard and races away. I consider pursuing him but not seriously. At the best of times, chasing a horse is hard work. I am in no condition to do so after a battle.

I look to the wolf, curious to see what he will do. He spends several long moments staring after the Supreme Huntmaster and scanning the courtyard for other dangers. Then, his pale blue eyes settle on me, and he lays down on the ground and yawns. Finally, he rests his head on his paws, closes his eyes, and initiates the change. His transformation to human form happens over the span of several seconds.

He forms on his side, slowly uncurls his body, and stretches. Spotting me, he grins.

"Hello, Katrina."

I assume my human form so I can ask him how he knows my name, but the words die in my throat when I see his face. The shape of his eyes, the slope of his nose, and the amused grin make him look exactly like my father—our father.

"I am called Adam. We've got a lot to catch up on, but we should take Vic's father to her."

Questions pile up, never fully forming, but I have enough sense to shake my head.

"He could die any second," Adam insists.

"He also weighs twice as much as Vic," I argue. "Wait here." Utilizing dog form, I dash back to where the others wait with Vic.

"Is everything all right?" Tellen inquires.

"Is my father …" Vic's voice falters and she swallows hard.

"He is safe for now," I answer, once back in human form.

"We should take her to him quickly." Shadow's eyes hold a distressing amount of worry.

Thankfully, Vic is not in the right position to read his eyes.

"I'll help you carry her," Tellen offers.

Shadow shakes his head and scoops Vic's slight body off the ground. She looks like she wants to argue but simply cannot afford the emotional energy that would take.

Not wanting to look into Vic's sad eyes, I lock gazes with Tellen. Wordlessly, he takes my hand and walks with me a few steps behind Shadow. Our somber procession emerges from the confines of the castle-like structure into the courtyard to find my brother leaning over Vic's father, head tilted close to his mouth to listen. The ropes that had once bound Vic's father litter the ground. Shadow covers the last few steps at a trot and carefully settles Vic next to her father.

"Vic!" Daniel Saveron whispers, trying to smile. His effort fails as his strength goes into fighting for another breath. "You. Were. Chosen." His next effort to smile succeeds as his eyes slowly close.

"Daddy? Don't leave me," Vic babbles. "I can save you!" She places her hands on his shoulder and drives off the poison with bursts of light from her bracers, but it is too little, too late.

The effort earns enough strength for her father to reach over and close his right hand around her left bracer. He spends his last few seconds staring up at her, trying to convey the many messages he has no time to deliver.

"I can try to save him," Shadow offers hesitantly.

"Then, do it!" Vic snaps, glaring at Shadow.

Releasing my hand, Tellen too levels a nasty look at Shadow.

"That's not an option."

"What are you talking about?" I ask Tellen.

"There's a healing ritual that can transfer blood between

people, but it doesn't always work, it must be done between blood relatives, and it's very dangerous," Tellen explains. He looks like he wants to murder Shadow for making the suggestion. "Vic could die."

"I don't care. Just do it," Vic orders. "What should I do?"

"Vic, don't," I plead, my heart breaking.

"Why not?" Vic fires the question like an arrow. "He's my father. I have to do something!"

I want to keep silent and let her do what she needs to do, but deep down I know the battle we just fought is only the first of a wider war.

"You were chosen." Tears pour down my face, and I feel horrible for echoing her father's last words.

"If I'm truly chosen, then I'll live through the experience," Vic says grimly. "And if I die, another will be chosen."

Sara's soft voice chimes from behind us.

"Ye should never test the One, but I think she may be right this time."

We turn and watch as Sara comes up half-supporting Ederon.

Letting Ederon slip gently down to the ground, Sara draws near.

"The first part of the prophecy says the Chosen Redeemer must suffer, and the second part speaks of defying death."

"How do you know?" I challenge.

"I know precious little more than anybody, but we will never win the coming war if our Chosen Redeemer is broken before it begins."

I hang my head and acknowledge the truth. The others nod slowly, and Vic nods grimly.

Shadow and a very reluctant Tellen perform the ritual over the course of the next few minutes, transferring fresh blood from Vic into her father's still form.

We wait and wait.

By the end, Vic's face looks as pale as the bright portal.

After the ritual, Tellen checks Vic's father for signs of life. Under instructions from Shadow, Adam chafes Daniel Saveron's wrists, attempting to get his blood flowing again. Sara breathes quiet prayers in our ears. Unconsciously, I hold my breath while Shadow gently squeezes Vic's arm.

"Please live," I say, voicing our thoughts. My gaze bounces between Vic and her father, unsure of who to watch.

Shadow and Tellen perform a ritual

Vic's father moans, lightening our hearts.
"Please, please live," I repeat, my attention now fixed on Vic.
We wait.

Utter stillness settles among us.
We wait some more.
At last, as my heart prepares to burst with worry, Vic awakens.

THE END

Thank You for Reading:

I hope you enjoyed the first adventure featuring Vic, Katrina, and Tellen. The saga continues in *The Holy War*. If you're wondering what went on before this story, check out *River's Edge Ransom* and the Aeris Legends stories to learn more about the events that shaped Daniel, Marina, Jordan, Christa, and Marcus.

Aeris stories in order: *River's Edge Ransom*, *The Huntsman and the Healer*, *The Dark Man's Wrath*, *The Lady's Grace*, *Awakening*, *The Holy War*, and *Reclaim the Darklands*.

Please visit my website: **www.juliecgilbert.com** to find a link to the current free works. Check out the audiobooks. They each have fantastic narrators. Or try a paperback. There's something wonderful about holding a physical book with pages to turn.

I would love to connect via email:
devyaschildren@gmail.com

Sincerely,

Julie C. Gilbert

www.ingramcontent.com/pod-product-compliance
Lightning Source LLC
Chambersburg PA
CBHW070756120626
46557CB00002B/616